A CHIEFTAIN FINDS LOVE

Barbara Cartland

Barbara Cartland Ebooks Ltd

This edition © 2017

ISBNs

9781782139492 ~ EPUB

9781782139508 ~ PAPERBACK

Book design by M-Y Books
m-ybooks.co.uk

THE BARBARA CARTLAND ETERNAL COLLECTION

The Barbara Cartland Eternal Collection is the unique opportunity to collect all five hundred of the timeless beautiful romantic novels written by the world's most celebrated and enduring romantic author.

Named the Eternal Collection because Barbara's inspiring stories of pure love, just the same as love itself, the books will be published on the internet at the rate of four titles per month until all five hundred are available.

The Eternal Collection, classic pure romance available worldwide for all time .

THE LATE DAME BARBARA CARTLAND

Barbara Cartland, who sadly died in May 2000 at the grand age of ninety eight, remains one of the world's most famous romantic novelists. With worldwide sales of over one billion, her outstanding 723 books have been translated into thirty six different languages, to be enjoyed by readers of romance globally.

Writing her first book 'Jigsaw' at the age of 21, Barbara became an immediate bestseller. Building upon this initial success, she wrote continuously throughout her life, producing bestsellers for an astonishing 76 years. In addition to Barbara Cartland's legion of fans in the UK and across Europe, her books have always been immensely popular in the USA. In 1976 she achieved the unprecedented feat of having books at numbers 1 & 2 in the prestigious B. Dalton Bookseller bestsellers list.

Although she is often referred to as the 'Queen of Romance', Barbara Cartland also wrote several historical biographies, six autobiographies and numerous theatrical plays as well as books on life, love, health and cookery. Becoming one of Britain's most popular media personalities and dressed in her trademark pink, Barbara spoke on radio and television about social and political issues, as well as making many public appearances.

In 1991 she became a Dame of the Order of the British Empire for her contribution to literature and her work for humanitarian and charitable causes.

Known for her glamour, style, and vitality Barbara Cartland became a legend in her own lifetime. Best remembered for her wonderful romantic novels and loved by millions of readers worldwide, her books remain treasured for their heroic heroes, plucky heroines and traditional values. But above all, it was Barbara Cartland's overriding belief in the positive power of love to help, heal and improve the quality of life for everyone that made her truly unique.

AUTHOR'S NOTE

On my sons' estate in the North of Scotland, a Viking ship is buried at the side of the River Helmsdale. Now covered with trees, one can only distinguish the outline of what was once a marauding vessel that terrorised the local inhabitants of the Strath.

The term 'Viking' is applied today to Scandinavians who left their homes intent on raiding or conquest during a period extending roughly from 800 AD to 1050.

In England, Viking raids began in about 780 AD and ended in 802, beginning again in 980 and the country ultimately became part of the Empire of King Canute.

The Viking threat ended with the ineffective King Canute II in the reign of William I.

From around AD 900 there were Viking settlements in the Orkney Islands, the Hebrides, Caithness in Scotland, Iceland and in the Faroes.

The Orkneys were not formally annexed to Scotland until 1772.

The power of the Earls of Orkney waxed and waned, sometimes encroaching on the mainland of Scotland, the Shetlands and the Hebrides and sometimes losing what had been gained.

Scandinavians abounded in the Hebrides and the Isle Man, and from time to time the Vikings claimed Kingship in those areas.

Yet, the establishment of a strong Royal line in the Isle of Man, although due to a Scandinavian, Godred Crovan, belongs to the second Viking period from 1079.

CHAPTER ONE
1885

Isa McNaver walked blithely along the seashore.

The sun was warm on her head and the wind just moved her hair off her forehead.

Because there was nobody to see her, she wore nothing on her head and, having taken off her shoes, carried them in her hand.

She could feel the wet sand and the waves lapping gently over her feet.

She thought as she had so often before that there was no place lovelier in the world than Scotland.

Most particularly the little bit of it that she thought of as her own because she had always lived there.

When she was away, as she had been during the last two years, she had never gone to sleep without thinking of the purple heather on the moors.

She dreamed of the mists over the distant mountains and the sea shimmering golden in the sunshine or silver in the moonlight.

'I am home! I am home.'

She wanted to cry the words aloud to the young gulls that flew overhead and the cormorants perched on the rocks jutting up above the surface of the sea.

She felt a little throb of her heart as she remembered that, if her voice did not recover quickly, she would have to go back to the South and find some other way of earning her living.

When she was seventeen and at school in Edinburgh, it was discovered that she had an exquisite soprano voice.

It had made her the leader of the choir in the local Kirk.

A theatrical impresario had quite by chance attended Morning Service there one Sunday and, having heard her sing, had asked the Minister to introduce him to Isa.

To her astonishment he informed her that she had a voice in a million.

He added that he was prepared to take her to London and produce her at a Concert that he was arranging where Her Majesty Queen Victoria would be present.

It was all like something out of a fairy story.

But Isa's parents were shocked and horrified at the idea of her appearing on a stage.

At first Colonel Alister McNaver had refused point-blank to consider such a proposition.

But when the impresario told him how much he was prepared to pay Isa, he was forced, because he was in desperate need of money, to agree.

Isa had finished her term at school and had then set off for London.

It was arranged for her to stay with one of her mother's sisters who had been no less horrified at the thought of any relation of hers being connected with the stage.

She, however, realised that Isa was singing in public solely in order to help her father and mother.

She was to be chaperoned from the moment she left the house until the moment she returned.

She never went anywhere unless she was accompanied by her aunt or else by her aunt's companion, who was if anything even more puritanical than her employer.

Isa was actually not in the least interested in the many invitations she received from the admirers of her voice.

In any case, whether they were young or old, rich or poor, they were not permitted to become acquainted with her.

The only people she was allowed to meet in London were her aunt's friends, who were mostly old and dull.

Also, as Isa thought secretly to herself, tone deaf.

However, she was a success!

During the last two years she had been able to send home quite a considerable amount of money earned from the Concerts arranged for her by the impresario.

They were not actually her own Concerts because she never appeared alone as he had a number of other protégés who also sang or played the piano.

There was a string quartet who, wherever they performed, drew the more experienced music lovers.

Then disaster struck.

Just before a Concert was to take place where she had been billed to perform, she developed laryngitis.

It was largely due to tiredness and her insistence on walking in Hyde Park on a cold blustery day that had brought on a streaming cold.

Under the circumstances there was no possibility of her appearing in the Concert.

And it was the impresario who had suggested that she took a holiday that she had not had since she first came to London.

She went back to her beloved Scotland.

Because he was so anxious for her to be fit to sing again as quickly as possible, he advanced the Railway fare for herself and an elderly housemaid whom her aunt insisted should escort her.

It had been a joy beyond words to see her parents again, although they now seemed much older than when she had left them.

The house on the hillside where her father's family had lived for generations was even shabbier than she remembered it.

However, because of the money she had been able to send them, the food was wholesome and good and there was plenty of it.

There were now two servants to wait on her father and her mother when before she left there had been none.

She had been longing to learn what they had been doing, to hear news of the lambing and whether it had been a good breeding season for grouse.

Stags were rare on their very small moor and so were the salmon her father managed to catch occasionally in the small stretch of river that ran through his estate.

It was all so familiar and at the same time so comforting that Isa felt as if she had never been away.

Now that she was home she had no wish to go back to London.

She knew, however, that this would be obligatory.

She therefore spent every moment she could walking along the seashore and climbing over the moors where the heather was just coming into bloom.

This morning when she woke up she had found that her voice had returned.

It was stronger and clearer than it had been for the last two weeks.

While she hummed a little tune to herself, she knew that it would be a mistake to try to sing too soon.

'I am better. Much better,' she thought.

At the same time it was an agony to know that now her voice had returned she must go back to the South.

She had walked quite a long way without realising it and was now beneath the cliffs.

There was on her left a huge cave that she remembered playing in when she was a child.

It had always fascinated her because somebody had told her that it had once been used by smugglers, although her father had pooh-poohed the idea.

"There has never been much smuggling in this part of the North," he said. "When the Vikings came, they put their longboats into one of the natural harbours and pillaged everything they could find."

Isa had been brought up on stories of the Vikings.

How they had carried off not only the sheep and cattle of those who lived near the sea but also the younger women. Besides this they had left in their wake a large number of fair-haired, blue-eyed babies.

They were very different from the small dark Picts and Scots who inhabited that part of the land.

"What is much more likely than anything else," Colonel McNaver often said, "is that the cave was used by the Scots to hide themselves and their families from the invaders."

That would have been a sensible thing to do, Isa had always thought, for the cave extended a long way back under the cliff.

She had also discovered that it was easy to climb up at the back of it and there she could lie on a kind of shelf beneath the stone roof and remain unobserved by anyone below.

Because she was thinking back affectionately into her childhood, she entered the cave now.

When she reached the far end of it, she climbed carefully with her bare feet up to the flat hiding place.

It now seemed a little smaller than she remembered it.

But she was sure that there would be room there for a man, his wife and perhaps two children together with some of their possessions..

She wished that she could read a story relating the feelings of the Scots when they saw from The Castle that was further to the North the first sign of the Viking ships coming across the North Sea towards them.

'It must have been very frightening,' she told herself.

She closed her eyes pretending that she was hiding from a Viking who would carry her away after stealing her father's flocks.

Perhaps, as a parting shot, they would burn down their croft.

Her eyes were still closed as she imagined it all happening.

Then astonishingly she heard voices below her.

For a moment or two she thought that she must be mistaken and it was just a part of her imagination.

Then, as she peeped over the edge of the rock where she was lying, she saw two men standing in the cave below her.

"I told Rory to meet us here," one man said in what seemed an unnecessarily low voice.

"What made you choose this cave?" the other man asked.

As he spoke, Isa realised that he was English.

The first speaker had a faint but undoubtedly Scottish intonation in his voice.

"It's the one place where we are out of sight of those *damned* stalkers," the first man replied. "You can never be quite certain that they are not lying up on the moors with a spyglass and you are being watched."

"I see your point," the Englishman said. "You are quite certain that we can trust this fellow Rory?"

"Not only can we trust him but he knows the layout of the land better than anybody else. As you well know, the map may not be very accurate after the passage of years."

"I am aware of that," the Englishman said. "At the same time there is no doubt of its authenticity."

He spoke sharply and the Scotsman replied in a conciliatory tone,

"My dear fellow, I am not disputing that, but even so it is very difficult to pinpoint exactly where the treasure is hidden."

At the word '*treasure*', Isa stiffened.

Now she realised what they were talking about.

Ever since she could remember, the Clan McNaver which her father belonged to had talked about the family treasure.

This had been hidden away somewhere when the Vikings approached.

Although they had left without it, the treasure had never been recovered and she was aware that the story was as familiar to every child in the Clan as the story of *Red Riding Hood* or *Cinderella*.

The Chieftain of the time, who had owned many acres of land along the Scottish shore, had been a man of great wealth and considerable ingenuity.

It was he who had built the old Castle that had stood high above the cliffs at the mouth of the river where it ran into the sea.

There he had lived, or so the story went, as if he was a King.

All the other Clans in the vicinity were afraid of the McNavers and had long since given up trying to fight them because they invariably lost.

The McNavers only enemies therefore were the Vikings, whose greed and seamanship brought them in the summer months to pillage everything they could find.

This meant that the McNavers were always on the watch for them.

At the first sight of the sails of the longboats on the horizon the sheep and cattle would be driven away over the moors.

Most of the women and children would go with them and the rest would hide in caves along the shore or inland in the woods.

After several skirmishes a number of the Chieftain's best men had been killed since the Vikings had superior weapons.

The Chieftain had then given orders that they were all to hide following the principle that '*he who fights and runs away lives to fight another day*'.

He had organised their plan of action with great efficiency and when the Vikings returned they found nothing but a few empty crofts and a Castle that was abandoned.

It had also been depleted of goblets, ornaments and jewels.

The marauders had then moved North or South in search of finer plunder.

While the Chieftain of the Clan McNaver led his people so wisely that they flourished.

Then disaster struck.

The Vikings arrived again and as usual as soon as their sails were seen on the horizon the operation of hiding from them was once more put into practice.

The Chieftain himself always supervised the concealment of the treasure from The Castle.

This had grown more valuable year by year as gold had been discovered in one of the burns and amethysts had been found in one of the mountains.

The treasure, which was said to weigh a considerable amount, was hastily taken to a hiding place.

It was one that apparently had never been used before as there was always the fear that a Member of the Clan might be captured and tortured until he revealed the whereabouts of the special crate of treasure.

Perhaps on this occasion the Chieftain and his Elders who dealt with the treasure had more to carry than usual. Perhaps they were slower.

At any rate, when they came from the new hiding place where they had concealed everything of value, the Vikings had already landed.

Seeing the small party of men moving towards them, their archers shot them down.

Everybody who had been in charge of the treasure, including the Chieftain himself, was killed.

There was therefore no one left after the Vikings departed to reveal to the rest of the Clan where the treasure had been hidden.

It was a story that had fired the imagination of every McNaver boy and girl.

Isa could remember making plans with her friends to take a picnic and spend a day searching the land that surrounded The Castle.

They were certain that they would find a cave in which treasure had been concealed.

She used to tell herself stories of how she discovered it all by herself and was hailed as a heroine by the whole Clan.

Now it seemed incredible that the two men below her in the cave were talking about the treasure.

A few minutes later they were joined by a third.

"Good day to you, Rory!" she heard the Scotsman say.

"Guid day to you too!" Rory replied.

There was no doubt that Rory spoke with a very broad Scots accent and Isa wondered if the Englishman would be able to understand him.

"This is Rory who has promised to help us," she heard the Scotsman say and the Englishman's crisp reply was,

"That is good! I want you to take a look at this map."

There was silence and, because she was so curious, Isa raised her head a little and peeped below.

The two men had their backs to her and were now standing nearer the entrance to the cave.

Rory, who she could see was wearing a tattered kilt and the plaid of the McNaver tartan, was inspecting the map.

She longed, as she had never longed for anything before, to have a glimpse of it herself.

She was sure that it was not clear to Rory, for he stood for a long time in silence before he muttered,

"'Tis difficult, very difficult!"

"That is obviously meant to be The Castle," the Scotsman said, pointing with his finger at a point on the map.

"Aye, it could be, it could be," Rory agreed. "But 'tis no near enough to the road."

"I imagine the people who lived hereabouts all those years ago could not draw very accurately," the Scotsman commented.

"If you ask me, the treasure must be somewhere in The Castle grounds," the Englishman remarked, "and not, as it has always been assumed, on the moors."

"Mebbe so," Rory agreed, "but I canna find anythin' to make us sure that's the truth."

"If it is in The Castle grounds," the Englishman said, "surely it will be difficult to explore the site without the Duke being aware of it."

There was a pause before the Scotsman replied in a low voice,

"I have told you before, we don't want to deal with the Duke either before or after we have found the treasure."

"Are you suggesting," the Englishman asked, "that we eliminate him?"

"It should not be difficult, one way or another," the Scotsman replied.

Isa drew in her breath.

Having heard what the men were suggesting, she put her head down.

If they should see her spying on them, she too might be eliminated.

It was unbelievable and horrifying that, apart from the Englishman, these two Scotsmen should contemplate murdering the Duke who was their Chieftain.

She had been brought up to believe that every Scotsman revered his Chieftain as a father figure and he was therefore prepared to follow him and fight for him to the death.

Then Rory spoke again,

"I thinks I ken where this mark on the map might be."

"Can you show it to us?" the Englishman exclaimed excitedly.

"Aye, that I can, but we've to go there on a moonlit night for we canna take a light with us."

"That is true," the Scotsman agreed. "A light, if it was seen from The Castle, might alert some nosey parker that something untoward was happening."

His voice deepened as he added,

"You understand, Rory, that you shall have your share of any treasure we find, but we do *not* wish anybody else to be involved except ourselves."

"Aye, sir, I ken fine what you mean," Rory replied, "but I canna be sure 'til I look at the place more careful like in the daylight."

"Can you do that without attracting attention?" the Scotsman asked.

"Aye, I can."

"Would you mind, Rory, going outside for a second? I want to discuss this with my friend."

"Aye, sir, I'll wait ootside 'til you calls me," Rory agreed.

Listening, Isa knew that he must have walked out of the cave and for a moment there was only the sound of the soft lap of the waves.

Then she heard the Scotsman speak in a low voice directly below her.

This meant, she knew, that they had moved further back into the cave so that they would not be overheard by Rory.

"We will have to let him look first without us," the Scotsman said.

"Can you trust him?" the Englishman enquired.

"I think so and even if he does find the treasure, he can hardly move it all by himself."

"I think we are taking a risk in letting him have the map."

"Don't worry," the Scotsman replied, "it's not the original. I have put that under lock and key and this is a replica of it."

"That was astute of you!" the Englishman remarked.

"I thought it was safer," the Scotsman said. "I could not take any risks with something that is worth millions of pounds!"

"If it is, then the Duke will undoubtedly claim it for himself and his Clan," the Englishman warned.

"That is why, once we are in sight of our objective, he cannot be allowed to interfere."

There was a hard note in the Scotsman's voice that made Isa shiver.

"Are you prepared to finish him off with your own hands?" the Englishman enquired.

The Scotsman laughed and it was not a pleasant sound.

"I am not such a fool as that! In this part of the world a man can have an accident with his gun on the moors, tumble over the cliffs into the sea or fall from the tower of his Castle."

"I see what you mean," the Englishman said slowly. "At the same time it is a risk."

"Everything is a risk," the Scotsman pointed out. "But if we find the treasure, is anything else of any relevance?"

"No, of course not," the Englishman agreed, "and I am glad that I was wise enough to approach you in the first place when I realised the value of this map."

"I am very grateful," the Scotsman replied. "Shall we now tell Rory to go ahead and investigate the place where he thinks that the treasure might be?"

"Yes, of course," the Englishman agreed. "Then he must get in touch with us, or rather you, immediately. After that we can go and see if what was hidden all those years ago is still intact."

"Age does not deteriorate gold, silver or jewels," the Scotsman said.

There was a note of greed in his voice as he mouthed over the words.

"Tell Rory to get on with it," the Englishman said, "and give him some money to keep him sweet."

"I was hoping you would do that," the Scotsman said.

The Englishman gave a little laugh as if the suggestion was what he had expected.

Then Isa thought that they moved towards the entrance to the cave.

One of them gave a low whistle and a few seconds later Rory was with them.

"We have decided that you can go ahead, Rory," the Scotsman said.

"And here are a few sovereigns for any expenses that you may incur," the Englishman added.

"Thank you, sir, thank you," Rory murmured.

"Now we leave one by one," the Scotsman said sharply. "You go first, Rory. Keep to the shore and go beneath the cliffs so that you cannot be seen by anybody up on the moors."

Rory must have touched his bonnet with his forefinger and then moved away.

Then there was silence until the Scotsman said,

"Goodbye, old boy. I will be in touch with you as soon as Rory has anything to report. You are staying where you were before?"

"Yes, it is very comfortable and I shall be there until you send for me."

"Good. And I hope that will be in a day or so."

Isa thought that the Englishman then walked away in the opposite direction from Rory, in fact the way she had come.

Then there was silence.

She was just about to raise her head and look down to see if the cave was empty when she heard just a faint sound.

Perhaps the man had knocked his head against a rock, but it made her stiffen and lie rigidly still with her head down.

It would have been terrifying, she thought, if she had moved too quickly and he realised that their conversation had been overheard.

She was quite certain that the Scotsman would not hesitate to dispose of her as he intended to dispose of the Duke.

If he killed her and left her body where she was now, it was very unlikely that it would ever be found.

Alternatively there was the sea and there would be nobody to see her being drowned.

At last, after what seemed an interminable passage of time, she heard him move out of the cave.

Then, because she could not help herself, she raised her head.

She had a quick impression of a man of average size silhouetted against the sunshine on the sea before he walked away to the North, as Rory had done.

Because she was afraid that he might come back, she did not move for a very long time.

Then slowly she climbed down from the flat rock, finding it somewhat painful for her bare feet and was relieved at last to be walking on the soft sand.

She walked slowly step by step towards the mouth of the cave.

The tide was coming in and it would not be long before it reached the cave.

Now she moved quickly Southwards, praying that no one was watching to see where she had come from.

Because she was afraid she began to run to where in the distance she could see silhouetted against the moorland the roofs of her home.

Only as she neared it did she slow down and ask herself what she was going to do about what she had overheard.

'I will tell Papa,' she thought.

When she was a child, she had always turned to him for the solution to any problem.

And then she knew that it would be a mistake.

He was now much more frail than when she had left home and it would be unkind to worry either her father or her mother with such a momentous problem.

Moreover it suddenly struck her, as if a blow from a weapon, that their lives might be put in jeopardy.

The Scotsman, whoever he might be, was prepared to murder the Duke, who was the most important personage in the whole area.

It would then not trouble him in the least to dispose of an ageing Colonel and his wife.

They were completely unprotected except for two servants, who were nearly as old as they were themselves.

'Whatever happens,' Isa said to herself, 'I must not involve Papa in this.'

Then she knew that the only decent and sensible thing to do would be to warn the Duke.

But the thought made her laugh at her own presumption.

How could she, of no importance and no significance whatsoever, approach the Duke of Strathnaver?

He was the Chieftain of the Clan and, as she had been told ever since she was a child, in this part of the world he was King in his own right.

She had seen the Duke only once and that was the year before she went South.

It was when the games took place, as they did every year, at The Castle.

The McNavers came from miles around to participate or to watch the Highland dancing.

They could also take part in tossing the caber, in the running and the wrestling and, what every strong man amongst them most enjoyed, the tug of war.

In the tug of war it was a struggle of hamlet against hamlet until one became the winner of the year.

After the games, venison and an ox would be roasted on the green and the pipers would play without ceasing until it was time for everybody to go home.

The last time that Isa had attended the games was with her father three years ago.

The Duke had put in an appearance late in the afternoon, looking magnificent in the full Highland dress of a Chieftain.

There were the black cock's feathers in his bonnet and his white sporran was hung with three tassels held by a silver chain.

She had not been at all close to him and, when she asked her father why he did not speak to the Duke, he had replied,

"The answer is quite simple, my dear, I am not important enough – a mere member of the Clan."

Because she was curious, Isa had asked questions.

She found that, although the Duke entertained lavishly at The Castle with large parties for shooting and fishing, he never included any of the locals.

There was, she learned, a certain amount of resentment because of this.

It had not troubled her herself, but she had felt that it was insulting to her father, who had commanded a Battalion of the Black Watch and won the Medal for Gallantry when he was serving abroad.

Her mother too was related to the Chieftain of the Hamiltons and she was very proud of her lineage, even though they were a Lowland Clan.

'Well, if we are not good enough, we are not good enough,' Isa told herself philosophically.

At the same time she would have liked to see the inside of The Castle, which she was told was very impressive.

It stood high above the sea surrounded by magnificently kept gardens and protected from the winter winds and snow by tall fir trees.

Now she told herself as she walked home that she could not possibly be brave enough to arrive uninvited at The Castle and tell the Duke what she had just overheard.

Then she asked herself how she would feel if he died suddenly and mysteriously.

Could she live with the knowledge that she could have saved him if she had wished to do so?

She argued with herself all the way until she reached the garden gate she had walked out from onto the moorland.

Then her chin went up and she told herself that, whatever else she might be, she was not a coward.

She was not afraid of the Duke. Why should she be?

'I will not say a word to Mama or Papa,' she decided, 'but I will ride over to The Castle tomorrow to tell the Duke what I overheard in the cave. After that he can look after himself!'

She did not realise that she tossed her head in a defiant little gesture as she reached her decision.

Then, as she moved through the garden and up towards the house, she was holding her chin high with a pride that was in her blood.

CHAPTER TWO

The Duke of Strathnaver threw himself down in a comfortable chair.

"Four before breakfast," he said, "and two more now. That is not bad for a morning's fishing!"

"You might have told me that you were going out so early," his friend the Honourable Harry Vernon complained.

"My dear fellow," the Duke answered, "you were so tired last night after that exhausting journey that I thought it would be sheer cruelty to drag you out at such an early hour."

"I admit I cannot really see the attraction of rising with the dawn," Harry said.

"Virgin water, my dear boy! The early bird who gets to the river before it is disturbed by other fishermen, dogs, cattle, stags, anything you like to name, has a better chance of catching, in this case, his salmon than anyone who comes later."

"You have certainly proved your point," Harry smiled, "and I shall try to equal your catch this afternoon."

"I shall be extremely annoyed if you do!" the Duke said and they laughed.

They were both exceedingly good-looking.

They had become friends when the Duke's father had surprisingly sent his only son not to Edinburgh, as he had been advised by his Elders, but to Eton.

He had wisely realised that it was time that Scotland began to open it borders and its industries to the South and he had been aware that the tradition of keeping themselves to themselves had already damaged the economy of the country.

Such a policy would make the majority of the landlords more poverty-stricken than they were already.

The Duke was in the fortunate position of having married a wife with a very large dowry.

Because he was extremely astute, he managed to make a profit from his tenants and his flocks as other Chieftains seemed unable to do.

A great deal of the land he owned was moorland. but there were other parts which were fertile and which he had been shrewd enough to develop either for grazing or for crops.

His only son, Bruce, was at first very unhappy in England.

He was used to being treated as if he was a Prince and having his own way in every particular.

When he tried to assert himself at Eton, he was kicked by his contemporaries. When as a 'fag' he had dared to answer the older boys, he was either bullied or beaten.

At first he thought of running away and then he decided that he would not be intimidated by anyone, especially Sassenachs.

He therefore set out to excel in games and nothing could have endeared him more quickly to an English boy's heart.

He played in the cricket First Eleven, he was Captain of the football team and, when he had time to row, proved himself a first class oarsman.

By the time he left Eton he was a member of 'Pop', admired and toadied to as a leader, and had also made a number of friends his father approved of.

His closest friend, the Honourable Harry Vernon, came from an old English aristocratic family.

Harry always spent his holidays in the early autumn at The Castle, looking on it almost as his second home.

If Bruce could offer him excellent grouse shooting, stalking and fishing, he in turn invited him in the Christmas holidays to one of the best pheasant shoots in England.

His father took him to Race Meetings where his colours were invariably first past the Winning Post.

The two young men went to Oxford University together and only when the Marquis served in the Cameron Highlanders were they separated.

A year ago the old Duke had died, his son had resigned from the Regiment and came North to take his place as Chieftain of the McNavers.

As this was the first time for six months that Harry had been able to join him, the young Duke, after long sessions with the Elders, and even longer ones with his factors, felt like a schoolboy at the start of his holidays.

"Now what have you planned for me?" Harry asked him.

"I am determined that you shall enjoy yourself," the Duke replied, "so today I have a party of beautiful young women arriving from England."

"Who are they?" Harry asked suspiciously.

"Lavinia Hambleton for me," the Duke replied, "and Dorothy Waltham for you."

Harry laughed.

"I don't believe it! How on earth did you persuade them to come so far North?"

"You really cannot be as modest as all that," the Duke replied mockingly.

Harry did not reply, but merely enquired,

"Do you intend to marry Lavinia?"

"I am in no hurry to marry anyone," the Duke answered, "although I realise that I must eventually produce an heir and my father was always bitterly disappointed that he had only one son."

There was silence and then he went on,

"At the same time is it possible that Lavinia would ever settle down in Scotland?"

"If you are asking me, you are expecting too much," Harry replied. "Lavinia is the most beautiful woman I have ever seen, but I have the feeling that, if you are sensible, you will marry a Scottish girl."

The Duke made a grimace but Harry went on,

"She will be used to the long winters, the endless conversation about sport and, of course, the inevitable complaints of the Clansmen over one thing or another."

The Duke rose from the sofa and moved towards the window with a serious expression on his face.

He looked out over the sea noticing the mist over the house and the warning lights to be seen on the hill that stretched out beyond The Castle.

Together with the small harbour that he could just see before him he thought that it was the most beautiful view he had ever seen.

And yet he was sensible enough to realise that for a woman it might be monotonous and boring.

It certainly did not include the glittering lights of London, the noise of traffic and the sounds of dance bands.

"If you marry," Harry said from behind him, "I advise a Scottish lass, who would be wildly excited because you had landed six salmon or if you managed to shoot a stag to fill the larder."

The way he spoke made the Duke give a short laugh.

Then he said,

"Have you ever met a Scots lassie who did not have thick legs, large feet and a face like a spinning wheel?"

Harry laughed and replied,

"I suppose you are a plain race where the womenfolk are concerned, while the men, like your father, are magnificent!"

The Duke glanced up at the portrait of his father that hung over the mantelpiece.

The fourth Duke of Strathnaver had been painted in the full regalia of a Chieftain with a plaid over his shoulder caught by a large silver brooch with an enormous cairngorm.

There was no doubt that he was a magnificent figure of a man.

"Even when he was an old man," the Duke said, "I remember thinking how handsome my father was, besides being awe-inspiring."

"As you will be yourself in thirty years' time," Harry said, "and extremely conceited about it!"

"If you talk to me like that," the Duke remonstrated, "I shall send you South and close my door to all Sassenachs!"

"I am sure that Lavinia will easily find somebody to console her," Harry teased him.

It struck the Duke that the answer to that was that nobody could be more important than he was himself. Then he thought that it would be a mistake to say so, even to Harry.

It was true that he found Lady Lavinia Hambleton alluring, exciting and more passionate than any woman he had ever met before.

The daughter of the Marquis of Dorset, she had been married when she was very young to a husband who had no idea how to control her.

Then after four years of marriage he had conveniently died of typhoid fever after being sent on a Military mission to India.

Lady Lavinia had not pretended to be inconsolable, she had merely looked lovelier than ever in mourning.

She was even more beautiful when she could wear soft shades of mauve and a deep purple that made her skin seem dazzlingly white.

At twenty-six she was at the height of her beauty.

When she saw the Duke, she could imagine that no man could be more suitable to be her husband and a complement to herself.

The Duke was aware that she was merely waiting for him to say the four words that would make her a Duchess.

But some instinct of self-preservation or perhaps it was his native Scottish caution, prevented him from committing himself.

Their *affaire de coeur* had lasted long enough for all the gossips to be aware of it.

Harry was thinking that an invitation to The Castle was tantamount to asking for her hand in marriage.

Because he was devoted to the Duke and felt like a brother to him, he was exceedingly anxious that he should marry the right woman.

He was perhaps the only person who was aware that the Duke had many hidden depths to his character.

He was also far more vulnerable and idealistic than he appeared to be. Equally he could be frighteningly authoritative when he chose.

There was no doubt that as he grew older he would rule his Clan in the autocratic way that his father had done.

Because Harry was English and had moved always amongst the great aristocratic families, he was aware of how important the Head of a Family could be.

His own father for instance was admired and revered by those who worked and lived on his estate.

Yet it was nothing, he often thought, beside the power and prestige of a Chieftain in Scotland.

Whilst the Chieftains no longer had the power over life and death, they still had an authority that seemed at times almost God-like.

Equally their Clansmen trusted and obeyed them as if they were actually their fathers.

The whole arrangement had always fascinated him.

He thought now that it was essential if the Duke was to be happy that he should marry a woman who would appreciate his position.

It was after all very different from that of an ordinary man.

Lady Lavinia was beautiful, there was no doubt about that.

She was also capable of making a man's heart beat faster and igniting within him a burning fiery desire.

But had she anything else to offer? It was a question that he thought was important.

Dorothy Waltham, whom the Duke had invited for him, was a very different proposition.

She was entrancing, witty and amusing and Harry found her physically irresistible.

Her husband, Sir Douglas, was forty years older than his wife and only interested in his duties at Court.

He was a Lord-in-Waiting and his special duty, because he was a good linguist, was to look after the Ambassadors. They arrived from all over the world to pay their homage to Queen Victoria.

He in fact found it a nuisance when his wife accompanied him to the functions that he organised. Then he had to concentrate on her as well as all the foreign guests of Her Majesty.

Dorothy Waltham was therefore left very much on her own and Harry had found it very easy to spend a great deal of time in her company.

It was typical, he thought now, that her husband allowed her to come to Scotland without him.

He would doubtless never give a thought as to whether she was or was not faithful to him while she was away.

He was a dull conscientious man, erudite, but with no imagination. From a social point of view because Sir Douglas was very rich it had been a brilliant marriage for the younger daughter of penniless country Squire.

Dorothy would have been exceedingly bored, however, if her beauty had not made her one of the most admired and sought after women in London Society.

The Duke turned from the window.

"To keep Lavinia and, of course, you, Harry, amused I have decided to give a ball here on Thursday night."

"A ball?" Harry exclaimed in surprise.

"Do you realise it is something that has never happened for the last twenty years?" the Duke asked. "I sent out the invitations a month ago and all the large houses within driving distance are having house parties for it."

"Good Heavens! I had no idea that such festivities were possible in this out of the way spot!"

"Are you being rude to me?" the Duke enquired.

"On the contrary," Harry replied, "I am congratulating you on your expertise in galvanising the Scots into being frivolous."

"What you are saying," the Duke remarked, "is that it is a change from shooting and fishing."

"Exactly!" Harry agreed. "And doubtless they will talk about it for the next one hundred years."

"It will in fact be quite a modest ball since my guests must all be within reasonable reach," the Duke said. "At the same time it will be amusing to see a hundred people dancing in the Chieftain's Room. I suppose you have not forgotten how to dance a reel?"

"You insult me," Harry protested. "But I must admit that in the past I was not always as good as you at it."

"Anyway it will give them something to talk about," the Duke smiled, "and I suggested to Lavinia when I wrote to her that she and Dorothy should take some lessons so that they will not feel out of it."

"I congratulate you," Harry exclaimed. "You seem to have thought of everything!"

"I have tried to, including having an orchestra sent up from Edinburgh and ordering my own pipers to give a performance which will surprise the Chieftains of the other Clans."

"If you had warned me, I might have bought myself a kilt," Harry said. "I know I have some Scottish blood somewhere in my Family Tree, but as it is, you and your fellow Scots all dressed up in your plumage will make even the smartest women look like Cinderella!"

"I am quite certain that Lavinia and Dorothy will look fantastic," the Duke said with satisfaction.

As he spoke, he walked to the grog tray which stood in a corner of the room saying as he did so,

"I am sure you want a drink."

"I will wait until luncheontime," Harry replied.

The Duke looked at the clock over the mantelpiece.

"It is not for another half an hour."

"I am keeping my head clear for this afternoon," Harry smiled, "for I have not forgotten that you are six fish ahead of me. In the past, however, I have often been lucky, if not as skilful as you."

"I bet you a sovereign that you do not catch six before five o'clock," the Duke countered.

"Done!" Harry replied. "But you will have to eat quickly for the sooner I get to the river the better."

"I suggest that you start – " the Duke began.

At that moment the door opened and a servant wearing a kilt said,

"There's a lady to see Your Grace!"

"A lady?" the Duke exclaimed. "Who is she?"

"Miss Isa McNaver, Your Grace. "

The Duke looked at his friend and said with a smile,

"That tells me nothing. Every person on the estate bears the same name!"

"All I can say is that the Postman has my deepest sympathy!" Harry replied.

The Duke laughed and said to the servant,

"What does this lady want of me?"

"I've no idea, Your Grace. She just says 'twas very important!"

"Oh, well, show her in," the Duke said.

The servant closed the door and he continued,

"I expect it is a complaint either about the Sinclairs in the North or the McGregors in the South. If it is not that, then the keepers have allowed their dogs to worry the sheep or else a wild cat is causing havoc among their chickens."

Harry laughed.

"World-shaking events! I can see that you are expected to be judge and jury in your Kingdom!"

"I have more important problems," the Duke said seriously, "but I will tell you about them later."

The door opened.

"Miss Isa McNaver, Your Grace," the servant announced.

As Isa came into the room, both men rose to their feet and there was an expression of surprise in their eyes.

The girl who entered looked very different from the type of Scottish lass they had expected.

She was wearing a pleated skirt of the McNaver tartan with a neat velvet jacket. Both were predominately green in colour and made her skin seem translucently white.

The hair under the small green hat she wore was vividly red.

Isa's hair was not the sandy red that was usual in Scotland, but the colour of beech leaves. It was streaked with gold and the sunlight made it appear vividly alive.

Her eyes were more grey than green and they too were flecked with gold.

As she stood looking at the Duke, both men thought that she might have stepped out of a picture.

It had only been yesterday evening when she was thinking over what had happened in the cave that she remembered that a year ago the old Duke had died.

It had slipped her memory because, when her father had written to tell her what had occurred, she had been busy preparing for a Concert that was to be performed at Christmas.

The rehearsals took place every day and she was not singing alone, as she usually did. She was a member of several groups and the soloist in the finale.

Everything had be sung again and again until she was so exhausted when she returned to her aunt's house that all she wanted to do was to go to bed.

Even her letters from home seemed unimportant beside the instructions she was receiving which were being altered and made more stringent at every rehearsal.

Now she recalled that her father had written to tell her that the old Duke was dead and had described the funeral in detail. He had attended it as every Scots within miles of The Castle had done.

The Duke had been carried by his relatives to the churchyard where generations of his family had been buried before him.

The pipers had played the lament that her father had said was very moving.

Afterwards there had been the wake where a large amount of whisky had been consumed.

Only the men of the McNaver Clan were present, as was usual in Scotland.

Because Isa had never attended a Scottish funeral, she found it hard to imagine exactly what it had been like.

Her father was not an eloquent writer and she supposed that was why she had completely forgotten what he had told her.

It was now the Marquis of Naver, whom she had not seen since she was a child, who had taken his place.

'Perhaps,' she thought, 'the treasure-hunters will think it easier to dispose of the new Duke than it would have been of his father, who was so awe-inspiring.'

Yet when she came into the room and was aware that she was facing the Duke, she thought that despite his youth he was in fact rather frightening.

Because he was as surprised by Isa as she was by him, there was silence until at last the Duke said,

"How do you do, Miss McNaver. I understand you wish to see me."

He held out his hand as he spoke.

As Isa took it, dropping him a curtsey as she did so, she wished that she had not come to The Castle.

She had been so certain that it was her duty to notify the Duke of the plot she had overheard.

It was only now that it struck her that he might think she was interfering or, worse still, not believe her.

"May I introduce my friend Mr. Harold Vernon?" the Duke asked.

Isa dropped Harry a small curtsey and then a little nervously she said,

"Perhaps – Your Grace – as what I have to say is – confidential – could I – see you alone?"

As he replied, there was a sarcastic twist to the Duke's lips as if he thought that she had some ulterior motive in wishing to be alone with him.

"Mr. Vernon is a very old friend of mine and however confidential your conversation will be, Miss McNaver, I wish him to take part in it."

Isa inclined her head and the Duke indicated with his hand an armchair.

"Will you sit down?" he enquired.

She obeyed him, sitting very upright, clasping her hands together in her lap.

The two men sat down and the Duke said,

"I don't think that we have met before. Do you live near here?"

"My father, Your Grace, is Colonel Alister McNaver – and lives at Kilphedir Lodge, which is about three miles South as the crow flies."

She spoke a little defiantly.

She was thinking of how her father and mother had never been invited to The Castle, although they lived so near.

"I know Kilphedir Lodge," the Duke said, "but I have not had the pleasure of meeting your father, or you, until now."

"No, Your Grace."

The Duke was aware there was an undoubted note of reproof in the monosyllable.

No one spoke and Isa was aware that they were waiting for her to begin.

With an effort she said,

"You may think it very – strange, Your Grace, but – yesterday I – overheard something so – unusual and so – odd that I felt it my duty to come and tell Your Grace what is being planned."

"Planned? By whom?" the Duke asked.

"By three men, Your Grace – whom I overheard talking when I was in a cave on the shore, which is about a mile from my father's house."

"What were you doing in the cave, Miss McNaver?" the Duke asked.

There was something in the way he spoke that told her that he had already made up his mind that her information was of little consequence.

Once again she wished that she had ignored what had happened and had not come to The Castle.

What was more, it was very difficult to explain that she was exploring the cave because it was something that she had done as a child.

"When I went – into the cave," she said in a low voice, "I walked to the back of it. I climbed up onto a flat ledge of rock – which is just below the roof."

She saw the Duke glance at Harry and, feeling sure that he was bored, she went on quickly,

"It was then that two men came into the cave."

"They could not see you?" Harry asked, as if he grasped the situation better than the Duke.

"Nobody knew that I was there," Isa replied.

Haltingly, because she felt uncomfortable, she recounted what she had heard the Scotsman say, while the Englishman had produced a map before they were joined by a younger man called Rory.

The Duke did not interrupt or ask questions.

He merely sat back in his chair, an expression of resignation on his face, as if he was compelled to listen to a story that he was quite certain was untrue.

It was only when Isa related how the Scotsman had said that the Duke must not be allowed to interfere and the Englishman had enquired if he intended to kill him with his bare hands, that Harry expostulated,

"Are you saying that they intend to *kill* His Grace?"

"The Scotsman said that a man can have an accident with a gun on the moors, tumble into the sea or fall from the tower of his Castle!"

"Great Heavens, I suppose that is true!" Harry exclaimed. "What are you going to do about it, Bruce?"

"To be honest," the Duke answered in a bored voice, "I think Miss McNaver was dreaming. It is impossible after so many years have elapsed for anybody to be concerned with a treasure of which there is no proof that it ever really existed in the first place!"

There was such a note of contempt in his voice that Isa flushed and rose to her feet.

"I am sorry, Your Grace, to have bothered you," she said, "but I only did what I thought was my duty in the circumstances."

As she spoke, holding her head high because she was angry, she walked towards the door.

She had almost reached it when Harry said,

"Please wait a moment, Miss McNaver, you cannot leave like that. You have told us what the three men said. Can you not identify them in some way?"

"Perhaps His Grace will be able to do that – if he is interested," Isa replied coldly.

Her hand went out towards the doorknob, but Harry rose from his seat and came towards her.

"I beg you, Miss McNaver," he said, "don't leave us when there are still a hundred questions I want to ask."

Isa did not reply and merely turned to look at the Duke. He too had risen from his chair and was standing with his back to the fireplace.

She knew without him speaking that he did not believe a word of what she had told him.

"Bruce, do persuade Miss McNaver to tell us more," Harry said.

"There is nothing I can add to what I have already told you," Isa answered. "They gave Rory some money, the Englishman turned South on leaving the cave and after an interval of time the Scotsman went in the other direction as Rory had done."

"And you say that they had no idea that you were listening?"

"None, Your Grace. I was careful not to make a sound because I was frightened."

"That they would dispose of you?"

There was a cynical note in the Duke's voice that told her he thought that she was hysterical.

She therefore turned again to the door, but Harry was standing in front of it.

"Of course you were frightened," he said. "If they had found out you were listening to their scheming, it is doubtful if they would have allowed you to escape to tell the Duke what was being planned."

"I-I was very frightened," Isa admitted, "and, when I reached home, I wanted to tell my father."

"Surely he was the first person you should have consulted," the Duke remarked as if he wished to find fault.

"I thought of it, but because the men sounded so determined that they would not be interfered with by you, Your Grace, I realised that my father and mother, who are both getting old, are also very vulnerable."

"I find it hard to credit," the Duke said, "that these men can intend to go about the countryside killing people indiscriminately, simply because they believe that they are on the track of some mythical treasure, which I personally have never believed in."

"I cannot see why not," Isa replied. "After all, it is a tale that has been handed down for generation after generation."

She drew in her breath and went on,

"I have always understood that your great-grandfather who rebuilt The Castle as it is now on the old site, often spoke longingly of the treasure which was never found and for which so many people have searched only to be disappointed."

"Disappointed because it is not there!" the Duke said sharply.

"That is your opinion," Isa said, and now there was an angry note in her voice. "But it is a story that is part of our history and I do not believe that there is a McNaver alive who would not be shocked if they knew that Your Grace thought it merely a figment of the imagination!"

Her voice seemed to ring out.

The Duke was aware that Harry's eyes were twinkling because this slim girl with her strange red hair was brave enough to confront him.

"If I *am* prepared to believe both in the treasure and also in these peculiar and unscrupulous men," the Duke said, "what do you suggest, Miss McNaver, I should do about it?"

"I have no idea, Your Grace," Isa said coldly. "At least if you die unexpectedly your blood will not be on *my* hands."

"On the contrary," the Duke pointed out. "You are the only person aware of my enemies, so if I die because you have not been able to identify them, I imagine that it will be on your conscience for the rest of your life."

Isa was still.

"What does Your Grace – mean?" she enquired.

"What I mean," he said, "is quite simple. You have heard these men speak, you realised that one of them, though you don't know his name, is a Scotsman and you have heard another voice you are ready to say was English. That would be some guide to their identification."

"Are you suggesting, Your Grace, that I find these men for you?"

"Of course," the Duke replied. "What else can you do, unless you are prepared, like Pontius Pilate, to wash your hands of me?"

Isa's eyes seemed to sparkle with anger.

"As Your Grace is making a joke of the – whole thing," she retorted, "I can only repeat that I have done my duty and I now hope to forget the whole episode."

"That is something you will be unable to do," Harry said quietly. "However much you may try to forget, you will wonder every day and every night from now onwards whether the three men have found the treasure and if they have disposed of the Duke."

"It is not my business," Isa insisted.

"As a member of the McNaver Clan," the Duke replied, "you know as well as I do that we are indissolubly linked together by blood, by tradition and by the obedience that every Clansman owes to his Chieftain!"

Now he was speaking quite sincerely and Isa stared at him as if she could hardly believe what he was saying.

Then because the very quietness of the way he spoke was somehow more intimidating that his cynicism, she asked helplessly,

"What – can I – do?"

"Leave that to us to decide," Harry interposed, "but please, come back and sit down. You know perfectly well that we cannot allow the Duke to be killed in cold blood just because he is too stupid or too brave to admit that he is in danger."

"Really, Harry!" the Duke expostulated.

"It's true, Bruce! Do you not see that it is true and that you are being extremely stupid? Of course Miss McNaver was absolutely right to come and tell you what she overheard."

The Duke made a murmur, but he did not interrupt as Harry went on,

"If these criminals really believe that they can get their hands on a treasure of such value, they would certainly kill you if you tried to interfere."

"You really believe that?" the Duke asked incredulously.

"Of course I believe it," Harry said. "Good Heavens, I have not read the history of this barbarous land or listened to you making my flesh creep with stories of your battles without realising how primitive the Scots still are in many ways."

"Thank you," the Duke said sarcastically.

"The person you should be thanking is Miss McNaver," Harry declared. "I personally think that it was very brave of her to come here and tell you a tale, which it would be easy for you to dismiss as fiction. And yet, if you are murdered, we could never forgive ourselves."

It flashed through Isa's mind that it would serve the Duke right.

Then she knew that Harry Vernon was talking sense.

It would be a disaster for the Clan if the Duke was killed when he had no direct heir to inherit.

She vaguely remembered that the Heir Presumptive to the Dukedom was a cousin who spent most of his time in London.

He was reputed to be extremely raffish and not in the least interested in his Scottish ancestry.

Suddenly because she loved Scotland and because it meant so much to her, she said in a very different tone from the one she had used before,

"Please – Your Grace – for the sake of the Clan, you must take care of – yourself!"

"That is exactly what I am trying to say," Harry agreed.

"You know as well as I do," Isa said, "that many Clans have lost their Chieftains who have gone South and forgotten their obligations and also that, owing to the Clearances, thousands of Scots were scattered and forgotten."

She drew in her breath as she added,

"If you die – everything might be – very different for the McNavers."

As she finished speaking there was silence.

She had no idea that because she spoke so beautifully and her voice was almost magnetic both men had been listening spellbound.

The Duke then capitulated.

"You are right, Miss McNaver," he said quietly, "and apologise for what I realise now was a very rude reception of what you had to tell me. Now, as my friend Harry has said, you must help me."

"I do not see how I can do that," Isa said quickly.

"It is quite simple," the Duke replied. "Somehow, in some way, you have to identify the three men you overheard talking in the cave."

"How can I – possibly do – that?" Isa asked with a helpless little note in her voice.

"I think the first thing for you to do," the Duke suggested, "is to come and stay here in The Castle. You will then be able to ascertain if the Scotsman is somebody close to me or someone perhaps actually living here."

Isa was astonished and her eyes seemed to fill her whole face as she stared at the Duke.

Then she asked hesitatingly,

"Are you – really asking me to – stay?"

"I have a number of guests arriving today," the Duke said with a smile. "If you are one of them, no one will be surprised, especially as I am giving a ball on Thursday."

"A – ball?" Isa exclaimed. "There has never been a ball at The Castle!"

"Well, now there will be," the Duke said, "and what could give you a better opportunity to observe my guests and perhaps identify the ones who intend to murder me?"

CHAPTER THREE

Isa stared out of the bedroom window at the lights that illuminated the garden and thought it looked like Fairyland.

Never had she imagined that she would ever be a guest at Strathnaver Castle.

It was a thrill to know that The Castle was looking more majestic and more impressive than she had ever seen it.

It was not only the pipers who greeted the guests when they arrived or the Duke's standard flying from the highest tower.

It was, she learnt, that the whole of the garden surrounding the building itself was to be illuminated with fairy lights and Chinese lanterns were to be hung from the trees.

She had been to a ball in Edinburgh and also several in London.

This, however, was particularly exciting because it was given by the Chieftain of her own Clan and she knew that a great number of his guests would be McNavers.

She had been disappointed that the Duke had not suggested inviting her father and mother.

Her father had at first considered it an insult that she was asked alone.

But when she explained that the Duke's grandmother was to play hostess for him, he and her mother could only relent and say that she was very fortunate to be included.

At the same time there was a little ache in her heart because her father had been ignored.

She thought that the Duke was proud, overbearing and too autocratic.

She had the feeling, although he said nothing to substantiate it, that he still did not believe her story.

She would in fact have been very perturbed if she had heard the conversation he had with Harry after she left.

They had both seen her off at The Castle door.

They had then been slightly amused, although they had not said so, that she had ridden over without wearing a riding habit.

She had thought that it would be somewhat embarrassing to walk about the house in a habit and hers was very old and threadbare as she had not been riding while she was in London.

When she was at home, if she wished to go somewhere on the moors or along the seashore, she would jump on the back of a horse just as she was without changing.

As her pleated skirt was very full, once she was in the saddle it would have been difficult for anybody who was not specially discerning to realise that she was actually not wearing a conventional habit.

She certainly looked exceedingly pretty in her green jacket, the sun glinting on her red hair as it showed under her small hat.

When she had ridden away out of earshot, Harry said,

"Well, that was a surprise! I did not expect to find anything so lovely as far North as this."

"You insult the Highlands," the Duke retorted and then added, "As a matter of fact I am as surprised as you are. I cannot think why I have not seen her before."

"You must have lost your eyesight," Harry laughed, "if you let that beauty pass by without your noticing it!"

They walked back into The Castle and the Duke said,

"I cannot help being amused at her ingenious way of getting asked to the ball."

Harry looked at him in surprise.

"Are you suggesting – ?"

"Of course I am!" the Duke replied. "She heard about the ball and was determined, one way or another, to procure an invitation."

"I must admit that it never crossed my mind," Harry said, "but I suppose it's a possibility."

"You are not usually so naïve," the Duke said mockingly, "but we shall soon see if she finds the 'villain of the piece' or what explanations she makes when there is no criminal and no treasure!"

"I think you are very cynical," Harry riposted accusingly. "I am quite prepared to believe her story from start to finish."

"Then I only hope you don't encourage her to stay for a month and have all the gardeners digging quite uselessly among the flowerbeds."

He walked off as he spoke and Harry looked after him with a slight frown between his eyes.

He had known that his friend Bruce was cynical where women were concerned and that he was also suspicious that they were running after him for his title.

But he had thought lately that the Duke was becoming even more sceptical.

He guessed the reason, only he had been hoping that it was not true.

Isa arriving home was excited and at the same time apprehensive.

*

If she went to the ball – which she knew was an irresistible attraction that she could not bear to miss – and saw nothing suspicious among the guests, she would feel exceedingly foolish!

The Duke would then be quite certain that the whole episode was part of her imagination.

'But it happened – it really happened,' she told herself reassuringly.

She was trying to decide whether to tell her father the whole truth or just say that she had been invited to stay at The Castle.

She was still frightened, even if it seemed ridiculous, that he and her mother might be hurt in some way.

She decided, although she hated lying, to invent a story.

She would say that she had met the Duke out riding and he had invited her to his ball.

She went over her story in her mind several times so that she would not make a mistake.

When she told her father and mother that there was to be a ball at The Castle and she was to stay there for it, they stared at her in sheer astonishment.

Finally they agreed that she could not refuse.

Then there was all the excitement of deciding what she should wear for such an auspicious occasion.

Fortunately Isa had brought with her two of the gowns that she wore when singing at the Concerts in London.

She had wanted to show them off to her mother, knowing how interested she would be. Now she thought with relief that she would at least be suitably dressed.

The ancient carriage that her mother used was made ready to convey her to The Castle on Thursday afternoon.

Because her mother thought it correct, their old maid was sitting on the small seat opposite her.

Isa thought that she had slipped back in time.

She had always been told that The Castle had been the focus for a great many other festivities when the Duke's great-grandfather was in residence.

It was he who had rebuilt the Castle and he had been in attendance on King George IV when he had visited Edinburgh and had astounded all his subjects by appearing in the full regalia of Highland dress.

The Duke had spent a fortune in modernising his Castle and had regularly invited a great number of the English as well as the Scottish Nobility to stay with him.

In those days they had come by sea and his small private harbour was large enough to hold their ships.

It was Bruce's grandfather who had succeeded him and who had to make economies to pay for his extravagance.

The present Duke was, thanks to his father's organising ability and his prudent marriage, a very rich man.

'He has everything,' Isa thought. 'What could be more satisfying than to own the most beautiful and certainly the most romantic Castle in the North of Scotland?'

She wondered if he felt the same about it and then she told herself that like so many of the Scottish young men he doubtless preferred the gaieties of the South.

Especially, she thought mockingly, the alluring women who were to be found in London.

Isa remembered that when she first appeared at the Concerts that were arranged for her, she was astonished at how beautiful the ladies in the audience were.

They were outstandingly elegant in their evening dresses.

Glittering with diamonds and usually wearing tiaras, to Isa, after the wilds of the Highlands and the Puritanical society she had met in Edinburgh, they were like something out of *The Arabian Nights*.

She had only vaguely heard of the professional beauties.

When she saw them in the audience, she understood how they had captured the imagination of the people. Postcards of them were on sale in the shops and people stood on the chairs in Hyde Park to see them drive by.

Once, when she had been singing at a special Concert which was attended by the Prince of Wales and Princess Alexandra, she had found it hard not to look at her audience like a child in a sweet shop.

She almost forgot that she was expected to sing.

Now, she thought, she might perhaps have a chance of meeting some of these beautiful women who were talked of by everybody in England from the lowliest shop girl to the much-acclaimed musicians she appeared with.

She had always been interested when she heard the Duke of Strathnaver being talked about in Scotland.

She was not surprised therefore when his name cropped up in conversation in London.

He was so good-looking that it was said that the Queen, who always liked handsome men, continually invited him to Buckingham Palace.

It was reputed that he had refused a position at Court because he believed that it was his duty to spend more time with his own people.

This was when his father was still alive.

When he inherited, he returned to Scotland and there was no chance of Isa seeing him at any of her Concerts. Nor did his name appear any more in the *Court Circular* of *The Times*.

Now that she was actually inside The Castle she realised that it was run to a smooth perfection.

Somehow it was something that she had not expected, but which she was sure that the Duke had learnt in the South.

On her arrival she stepped out of the old-fashioned carriage and left the maid who had accompanied her to go back to her home in it.

She entered The Castle to be looked after by a kilted Major Domo who was in command of a number of footmen.

He in turn passed her over to the housekeeper rustling in black silk with a silver chatelaine hanging from her waist.

There were two maids to unpack her trunk and she was in a bedroom that did not look out over the sea, but over the gardens behind The Castle, beyond which lay the moors.

The gardens were one of the great sights of that part of Scotland and the Duke contrived to grow a great number of different flowers and houseplants.

He had also used the cascade that fell down the side of the hill to create a Water Garden that, with its rocks and shrubs and small bridges, evoked the envy of every gardener North of the border.

Isa had read about the Water Garden of The Castle and now, she thought, she would be able to see it for the first time.

Opening the window, she could see the cascade. Brown with peat, it was splashing down to where it joined a burn which ran through the garden to fall over the cliffs into the sea.

On the other side of the gardens flowed the river that the Viking ships had sailed up when they crossed the North Sea for their raids on Scotland.

It had in those days furnished them with a harbour where they could disembark their warriors.

It was all quite fascinating and, as she stood looking out at the bright lights, the Chinese lanterns and a moon rising over the moors, she knew that nothing could be more beautiful.

It stirred her imagination so that, as she had often done before, she thanked God that she had been born a Scot and every nerve in her body responded to the beauty of the land of her birth.

She felt that she was so much a part of it all that she had no separate identity of her own and she could feel the whole history of Scotland pulsating in her mind.

She could breathe the heather-scented air and her eyes were illuminated by the silver loch in the distance.

The wind blowing in from the sea made her think of the Scots who had left their homes and settled in many different lands. However much they succeeded in their new lives it never compensated them for the home they had lost.

'Once a Scot, always a Scot!' she said to herself.

There was nothing in London that she loved in the same way as she loved the light on the hills when there was sunshine and the mists over the moors when the skies were dark.

With an effort she remembered that she was expected after dressing to go downstairs before dinner and meet her host and the other guests who were staying at The Castle.

A groom had brought her instructions to her home and they had been very explicit, so that there was no chance of her making a mistake.

She was expected to arrive just before it was time to dress for dinner.

When she had immediately been handed over by the Major Domo to the housekeeper, she had realised that she was not first to meet the Duke.

She thought with a little smile that he was being very autocratic and it was only surprising that she had not expected to ask for an audience with him.

Then she told herself that she would be wise to keep her sense of humour under control.

She was quite certain the Duke would not think it amusing if she did not treat him as the Chieftain.

As a Chieftain, this meant that on his own lands he was a King in his own right.

She took one last glance at herself in the long mirror.

Her gown, which had come from a very expensive dressmaker in Bond Street, was exceedingly becoming. Of white satin, its low décolletage, and she had at first been shocked at how low it was expected in London to be, was draped with chiffon.

There were flounces of chiffon around the hem, which formed a short train behind her when she walked.

And the pure whiteness of her gown threw into prominence the strange glowing red of her hair.

In it instead of diamonds, which she expected would be worn by most of the other guests, there was just a tiny white osprey feather, which fluttered when she walked and made her seem ethereal rather than of this world.

This was partly due to the fact that she was very thin.

Because she had taken so much exercise when she was at home in Scotland, she found it impossible, as so many musicians did, to rush straight to rehearsals without taking the air.

In London she therefore rose very early and would walk in Hyde Park, stepping out as if she was tramping over the moors. Deep in her thoughts she had no idea that people stopped to stare at her until she was out of sight.

Her aunt, however, had insisted that she was accompanied on her walks.

But no housemaid, however young, who was sent as a chaperone found it possible to keep up with Isa who resented having to slow down.

She therefore made an arrangement without her aunt's knowledge that the housemaid would wait for her on a bench in the Park.

Then she would walk quickly away and return to her in half-an-hour.

It was a subterfuge that the housemaid appreciated and provided Isa with the exercise she needed.

It also kept her slim and athletic and her gown moulded to her figure made her look very young and graceful and somehow unlike any other woman in the party.

Because besides the number of guests staying the night there were others from other houses in the neighbourhood, everyone was announced.

When she entered the drawing room, the Major Domo called out,

"Miss Isa McNaver, Your Grace."

For a moment Isa could see nothing but a kaleidoscope of colour and the glitter of jewels.

Then the Duke came towards her and she thought in full dress with a lace jabot at his throat and his plaid over one shoulder that no man could look more magnificent.

As he took her hand, he said,

"Welcome to The Castle!"

She then felt a strange vibration from his fingers that she had never experienced with any other man.

Then Harry was beside her saying,

"You look beautiful, as I expect you will be told a thousand times this evening, but I wanted to be the first."

Isa smiled at him.

Then, as the Duke's attention was transferred to a new arrival, Harry drew her across the room to introduce her to the Dowager Duchess.

Isa had not seen her except at a distance many years before and she now felt that with her white hair she looked more beautiful than any young woman could do.

The Dowager Duchess was wearing a mauve gown, the colour of the heather just coming into bloom.

Her tiara of amethysts and diamonds had been a present from the whole Clan when she had married the Duke and there were stones of the same gem around her neck and on her wrists.

It flashed through Isa's mind that it was jewels like these found in the mountains of Scotland that were in the treasure that had been hidden from the Vikings.

"It is a great pleasure to meet you, Miss McNaver," the Dowager Duchess was saying. "Do you live near here?"

"About three miles from The Castle, Your Grace."

The Dowager Duchess could not repress a little look of surprise and Isa knew that it was because her gown was so obviously smart and expensive.

It must seem strange to the Dowager Duchess, she thought, that she had not been invited to The Castle before.

Then, as Harry introduced her to one person after another, she realised that all the people staying at The Castle were either from England or else from the South of Scotland.

The Duke of Hamilton was wearing the tartan of the Royal Stuarts which he was entitled to and the

Duke of Buccleuch was equally resplendent in his own tartan.

If the men were magnificent, Isa's breath was taken away by the elegance of the women.

As she heard their names being announced, she recognised several of the great beauties like Lady de Grey and Lady Brooke.

She thought it would have been impossible for any women to glitter more brightly than the stars.

Yet the jewels on their heads and around their necks eclipsed anything she had seen before.

Then at last, when the room seemed to be filled to overflowing, they processed in to dinner and Isa found herself being escorted by a gentleman she was introduced to as Lord Durham.

He immediately began to pay her compliments, which she found somewhat embarrassing.

During dinner he expressed himself very volubly on the subject of how he enjoyed the company of beautiful women and made it quite clear that he put her in that category.

The gentleman on her other side was more prosaic, but amusing when she talked to him about sport.

She found herself fascinated by the huge dining room, the gold and silver ornaments on the table and the meal, which was really delicious in itself.

At the end of dinner when the port had been taken round, the Duke's piper circled round the table playing tunes that Isa had known since she was in the cradle.

She felt that the music was moving and very exhilarating.

She was aware, however, that some of the English guests made little grimaces at each other and put their hands up to their ears.

When the piper had finished, he stopped at the Duke's high chair at the top of the table.

The Duke handed him the special silver cup that was kept for the occasion and contained whisky.

The Piper drank his health, speaking in Gaelic.

When the ceremony was finished, the ladies left the room and Isa knew that a number of them were curious as to who she was.

They tried by asking tactful questions to ascertain if she was anyone of importance.

Only when they reached the Chieftain's Room did Isa remember for the first time that she should have been thinking of the real reason why she was at the party.

Because she had been so interested, she had forgotten that she was supposed to be listening to the gentlemen's voices.

Now she asked herself if one of the guests could be the man who was plotting to find the treasure and perhaps murder the Duke in the process.

When she had thought about it before she arrived, she had been quite confident, because she was so attuned to music, that she could not fail to recognise the way he had spoken.

It was nothing she could explicitly describe as being different from any other man's voice and yet there had been something about it that she felt she would definitely remember.

Now that she had entered the Chieftain's Room where the ball was to take place and saw the large number of men present in kilts, she was sure that it was like looking for a needle in a haystack.

The band was playing a soft waltz and she was immediately claimed by Harry and taken onto the floor.

He danced very well and she thought that he too looked exceedingly smart in his tailcoat and stiff white shirt.

It was difficult, however, not to compare him with the Duke.

He was not yet dancing, but receiving with his grandmother a number of other guests from various house parties in the neighbourhood.

"You are enjoying yourself?" Harry asked as they moved sedately over the polished floor.

"It is all like a scene from an Opera," Isa said, "and I find it difficult to believe it is real."

"That is what people are saying and thinking about you!" Harry smiled. "I find it impossible to believe that you spend much time in Scotland."

She was about to tell him that she was working in England when the dance came to an end and several people came up to talk to Harry.

There were other partners, in fact Isa was never without one, and, because it was a warm evening, they wandered into the garden.

Instinctively she moved towards the Water Garden and Lord Durham, who was her partner, looked at the cascade that fed it and observed,

"I am beginning to believe, lovely lady, that you have emerged from the cascade or else you are a mermaid from the sea who has become human for one night only!"

"I am delighted to be either, my Lord." Isa replied.

"You really are a McNaver?" he persisted. "If that is true, I cannot think why you have been allowed to remain hidden here in the hills instead of fascinating us all, as you should be doing, in the glittering lights of London!"

It seemed too much trouble to explain that that was exactly what she did.

She therefore let him continue to flirt with her as they walked back to The Castle and she was claimed by some other gentleman to take part in a reel.

As Isa had danced it ever since she was a small child, she had no difficulty with the complicated steps and looked exceedingly graceful as she did so.

Some of the other ladies were very clumsy in following the most intricate of steps.

Finally Isa found herself partnered by the Duke and, as they danced opposite each other, he said,

"Now I am prepared to believe that you really are a McNaver!"

"Why should you have doubted it?" Isa enquired.

"For a start, most of my Clan do not look at all like you!"

Then they both laughed because it sounded so funny.

They were parted and she did not speak to him again until the ball ended and the visiting guests had driven away.

Only the house party was left, some of the ladies looking tired.

Isa however, although she was not aware of it, was still sparkling.

"This is the best ball I have been to for a long time, Bruce," Lord Durham declared.

"Then I must certainly arrange another," the Duke replied.

"I shall look to Miss McNaver, as one of your Clan, to keep you up to that promise," Lord Durham smiled.

A middle-aged man whom Isa had not spoken to before joined in the conversation by saying,

"I have been puzzling all the evening as to where I have seen Miss McNaver before and somehow the name does not suit her."

Isa turned to look at him and, as she did so, he gave an exclamation.

"Now I have it!" he said. "You are Isa of the Isles! I listened to you just three weeks ago."

Isa smiled.

"At the Aeoleon Hall."

As she spoke, the Duke interposed,

"What is this you are saying?"

"Now at last I have remembered," the gentleman replied, "where I have seen this lovely lady before. She is not only beautiful but has a voice like an angel. She was so enchanting that I found I had been sitting on a very hard chair without complaining for two hours listening to her!"

Isa laughed.

Then she saw that the Duke was looking at her with a frown between his eyes.

As Lord Lovat turned away to say 'goodnight' to another lady in the party, he said in a low voice,

"So I was right! You were acting a part, Miss McNaver, and I can only congratulate you on thinking up such an original way of obtaining an invitation to my ball!"

Isa's eyes seemed to widen until they filled her whole face.

The way the Duke spoke and the sarcasm in his voice made her realise that he was being insulting, but for a moment she could not think why.

Then, as she realised what he was insinuating, the blood flooded into her face.

"If that is what you really believe, Your Grace," she said, "I can only assure you on my word of honour that it is untrue."

The Duke raised his eyebrows.

"And of course, Miss McNaver, I have to believe you," he replied.

His tone nevertheless told her only too clearly that he thought she was lying.

"I shall look forward," he continued, "to hearing tomorrow anything of interest that you have discovered here this evening, which I believe I am right in saying was the reason for your presence."

Because he was so obviously contemptuous Isa felt for a moment that she wanted to scream at him for doubting her.

She felt herself tremble and, although she was not aware of it, she went very pale.

It was impossible to speak, impossible even to refute the way that the Duke was accusing her.

As he turned on his heel and walked away, she did the same.

She left the room and, when she was outside it, she ran down the passage and up the stairs to her bedroom.

Only when she was inside and had closed the door behind her did she realise that her breath was coming quickly and her heart was beating tempestuously.

"How *dare* he! How dare he call me a liar just so that I could receive an invitation to his ball!"

She walked to the window to stand looking out.

Now the servants were extinguishing the lights that had edged the paths and hung from the trees.

The moon, high in the Heavens, was now throwing its silver light over everything, gleaming on the cascade so that it was turned to silver and casting strange shadows on the fir trees.

It was lovely, but Isa was looking out into the darkness and her fury seemed to make everything dark and ominous.

How dare the Duke talk to her in such a way? She regretted now that she had not said at the very beginning of their acquaintance that she was a singer and that she had returned home from London.

She had in fact tried to talk very little about herself, feeling that if she did so she would make it obvious that her father had felt neglected because he was not asked to The Castle.

The Duke had merely carried on the pattern set by his father, who had never thought it necessary to entertain his more lowly and unimportant neighbours.

She stood for a long time at the window forgetting that the maid who helped her dress had told her to ring when she returned to go to bed.

Quite suddenly Isa made up her mind that she would go home.

How, after the way the Duke had spoken to her, could she stay at The Castle and perhaps be obliged to meet him at breakfast?

He had made it very clear that he thought she was an imposter.

She would let him think what he liked, but in the circumstances she would no longer accept his hospitality.

Quickly, because she was angry, Isa took off her white gown and dressed herself in the clothes she had arrived in.

Because they had been the best she had brought with her from London, she put on the pleated skirt that she had ridden over originally in and the green velvet jacket that went with it.

She slipped on a pair of sensible walking shoes, did not bother with a hat, but took the osprey feather from her hair and laid it on the dressing table.

She wrote a note to the maid asking her to pack everything and said that she would send for it during the morning.

Putting the letter in an envelope with a tip, she left it on the unslept-in bed.

Taking one quick glance around the room, she opened the door quietly, realising that the passage was almost in darkness.

She thought that by this time the servants would have retired to bed and she was not mistaken.

When she reached the hall, there was not even a night- footman in attendance.

Very quietly she unbolted and unlocked the front door and stepped out.

It was easy to see her way by the light of the moon.

She knew, even though it would be a long walk home, that she would not find it difficult to make her way over the moors and it would at least be quicker than if she had been driving.

To reach the moors, however, she had to go through the garden and across the stream from the cascade.

There was, she knew, a small bridge built a little way from it.

As she moved over the smooth lawns and passed the flowerbeds, she kept wherever possible in the shadow of the trees for the moonlight was very bright.

It had taken her some time to change her clothes and write the letter and she was therefore not surprised to find that all the lights had now been extinguished in the garden.

Looking back she saw the lights in the windows of The Castle were also going out one by one.

She thought perhaps that the Duke would be surprised in the morning when he found that she had left.

Then she told herself that he was so sceptical that he would not worry in the least that she had felt too slighted by what he had said to stay any longer under his roof.

'I hate him!' she told herself. 'Papa and Mama were quite right and I should not have come in the first place. If those men kill him, it is only what he deserves.'

It was then as she moved towards the bridge, which she could cross the stream by that she heard voices and stopped.

There was a large fir tree just on her right and, because she had no wish to be seen or questioned, she slipped under its branches.

She stood with her back against the trunk, knowing that she would not be noticed by anybody looking casually at the tree.

It was unlikely that at this time of the night anybody would be curious enough to look too closely.

The voices came nearer, but they were low.

Suddenly Isa was alerted for quite distinctly she heard the Englishman whom she had heard in the cave say,

"You are quite certain, Rory, that you have searched everywhere indicated?"

"Aye sir, and t'was easy tonight with so many people aboot, and no one curious as to what I were a-doin'."

"You found nothing?"

"Nae, sir."

There was silence, then the Scotsman, and there was no doubt that it was the same man she had heard before, said,

"We are not likely to get another chance as good as this. But the map definitely indicates that the treasure should be about this distance from the old Castle."

"There is always the chance, I suppose," the Englishman said, "that it was uncovered when The Castle was rebuilt and the gardens created."

"My dear fellow," the Scotsman replied, "if a treasure of that magnitude and antiquity had been found, the very stones of Scotland would have talked about it! Nothing so important as that could be kept a secret for long."

"Assuming you are right," the Englishman said, "what do you suggest we do now, Rory?"

"I dinna ken, there's nae much we can do," Rory replied. "But I'll take another look around, if it pleases you, sir."

"Of course you have to do that," the Englishman replied sharply. "Tell him, McNaver, whether we are here or not, he will have to keep his eyes open."

"I was thinking," the Scotsman replied, "that The Castle was extended so tremendously and the gardens have taken up so much acreage that was not used before, that perhaps we are looking too far afield."

"We have been through all this before," the Englishman said with a note of impatience in his voice. "We have allowed for the new building, the gardens which then, as now, were bounded by this stream. We could, of course, look nearer to the cascade."

"That is going to be difficult as it is covered by the rock garden," the Scotsman replied.

"I know, I know," the Englishman agreed in an irritable tone, "but we can hardly give up now."

"No, no, of course not!" the Scotsman agreed. "Let me remind you that, as Rory and I are McNavers, we fight to the end. That is what our family motto has told us to do!"

There was a contemptuous note in his voice, but the Englishman merely laughed.

"Very well, go on fighting!" he said. "You and I know it is damned well worth the trouble."

"Of course!" the Scotsman said. "Now, Rory, what do you suggest we do?"

"I'll have another look round tomorrow, sir," Rory replied. "They'll want all the help they can get in cleanin' up the garden, and the house as well for that matter! Mabbe I'll have another idea then."

"When you have, let me know," the Scotsman said, "but be careful, for God's sake be careful, and keep your mouth shut!"

"I am sure he will," the Englishman interposed. "There will be a large sum of money waiting for him if he finds what we seek. Now I, for one, am going off to bed, Talbot, and you had better do the same."

"I suppose it's a waste of time to do anything else," the Scotsman said grudgingly.

They murmured something that Isa could not hear and then she was aware that they were all three crossing the bridge as she had intended to do and walking away.

She wanted to follow them, but was afraid that if she moved from the tree they would see her in the moonlight.

Only when they had disappeared in the distance did she very cautiously come out from below the boughs.

Nervously, she moved down some steps, which led her to the bridge that crossed the stream.

As she reached it, she looked back to where the cascade was roaring down behind the Water Garden.

Only then did she realise that, despite the Duke's sneers, she now had something to tell him.

Not only that the men had been searching during the ball for the treasure but also she had one important clue, the Scotsman's name was 'Talbot'.

There would, of course, be many Scots of the same name in the vicinity, but not so many who were well educated and spoke with only a faint accent.

She stood beside the bridge, which was made only of a few planks crossing the stream without a railing to hold on to.

Suddenly she decided that she was making a mistake.

Why should she run away? And if she did do so, would it not in the Duke's eyes prove her guilty of what he had accused her?

Her chin came up and her pride returned to sweep away the humiliation that she had been feeling because he had spoken to her so scathingly.

She would prove him wrong if it was the last thing she did!

She turned round and carefully retraced her steps. When she reached The Castle door she was afraid that somebody might have discovered that she had opened it and would have locked and bolted it again.

To her great relief, however, it was exactly as she had left it and she entered the hall.

As she walked up the stairs, moving quietly over the carpet, she reached the first floor and saw that the door was open into the drawing room where the Duke had received his dinner guests.

Without really meaning to, she looked inside.

Almost as if her thoughts had conjured him up, he was there, standing looking at her, the lights not extinguished but lowered, so that he was silhouetted against them.

His face was therefore in shadow, but what light there was showed hers very clearly.

For a moment they both stared at each other.

Then the Duke in the same contemptuous voice that he had used before said,

"Have you been looking personally for this strange elusive treasure, Miss McNaver? Or have you had a much more agreeable assignation in the garden?"

CHAPTER FOUR

Isa stiffened, then her temper rose and she replied,

"On the contrary. Your Grace, I have just found out something of importance that I think you should know. But if you are not interested, I can, of course, leave The Castle now, as I had intended to do."

She had no idea as she spoke that her eyes seemed to flash fire! And the light from the drawing room turned her hair to small leaping flames.

With a twist of his lips that made her even angrier than she was already, the Duke said,

"Perhaps you should come into the drawing room, Miss McNaver, where we can speak without being overheard."

He intended to make it a reproof.

But Isa walked ahead of him into the room holding her head high and feeling her anger rising like a flood tide within her.

Two lamps by the fireside lit the portrait of the Duke's grandfather over the mantelpiece and Isa looked up at it remembering that his blood flowed in her veins.

Although his grandson might be a Chieftain, she was a McNaver and afraid of nothing, not even of him!

The Duke closed the door behind him and walked towards her.

"Well, Miss McNaver," he asked, "what have you to tell me?"

"I was in two minds whether to go home as I had intended to do – "

"You were going home?" the Duke interrupted in surprise.

"Did you expect me to do anything else after you had been so insulting?"

"You intended to walk back to your parents?"

"As you see I am well equipped to do so," Isa said. "But then, when I was in your garden I changed my mind."

"Why?"

The monosyllable was sharp.

And she answered in an equally aggressive voice,

"Because I overheard some new evidence that I thought Your Grace should know."

"New evidence?"

Deliberately, hoping that it would annoy him, Isa sat down in one of the straight-backed chairs and forced herself to appear at her ease.

She had the feeling that the Duke was interrogating her as if she was a raw recruit or perhaps a Clansman whom he overawed.

She was determined not to be subservient to him and she said slowly,

"I was wondering whether to ignore what I had overheard and go home as I had intended. Then I remembered that it was not only Your Grace's life which was at stake but the honour of the Clan."

She did not look at the Duke as she spoke.

She reckoned that he would be twisting his lips in a way that had told her before that he did not believe her.

She was certain too that he would be looking contemptuous.

Suddenly she wished that she had not returned to The Castle.

The Duke could think what he liked and, if his treasure was snatched from him, he and those like him would realise how foolish they had been.

In fact perhaps, as the Scotsman had said in the cave, he would already have been disposed of.

"You speak of the honour of the Clan," the Duke said quietly, "and that, as you are well aware, is more important than either of us."

She glanced at him as if surprised that he could read her thoughts and then looked away again.

"I am waiting," he said after a pause while she felt for words.

"Very well, I will tell you what happened," Isa said. "I decided after your insults that I would return home and send for my luggage in the morning."

"I am sorry, Miss McNaver, and I am prepared to apologise, but you did not tell me you were an actress."

"I am not an actress!" Isa parried sharply. "I am a singer and the only stage I perform on is a Concert platform."

She felt that he was looking at her with even more contempt than he had before and she continued,

"I am not making any excuses, but when it was discovered that I had an unusual soprano voice, I felt that it was a way to help my father and mother who were extremely poor and in consequence were ignored by the Chieftain of our Clan, even though my father commanded a Battalion of the Black Watch."

"I can understand how it has hurt them," the Duke said quietly, "and it is certainly something that I will rectify."

Isa was too annoyed to be pleased by his promise and she merely went on,

"I accepted your invitation to the ball not, as you insinuated, to impose myself on you, but because I genuinely believed that you should know what was happening."

"I have already apologised," the Duke replied, "but, when Lord Lovat remembered that he had seen you in London, it came as a complete surprise."

Isa did not speak and he carried on,

"I understand that you did not use your real name."

"My father would not allow me to," Isa answered, "so when I sing it is as 'Isa of the Isles'."

The Duke nodded as if he understood and she then said,

"But this, Your Grace, is no concern of yours. What is important is that, when I was leaving a short while ago, I overheard in the garden the three men I had listened to in the cave. They have been searching the gardens where they think that the treasure is hidden."

"In the gardens?" the Duke exclaimed. "That seems very unlikely."

"As I told you before, they have a map of some sort. It must have been drawn when the old Castle was in existence and this present building is very much larger."

"What did they say?" the Duke asked.

"Rory said that, because there were so many people about, he had been able to search without arousing suspicion, but he had found nothing. But I did learn while they were talking the name of the Scotsman."

"That is interesting," the Duke commented. "What is it?"

"Talbot McNaver."

The Duke stiffened and now he stared at Isa as if he could not have heard her aright.

"You are quite certain?" he asked.

"Absolutely," Isa replied. "The Englishman addressed him as 'Talbo' and the Scotsman said when there was a question of giving up, 'let me remind you that Rory and I are McNavers. We fight to the end. That is what our family motto tells us to do'."

"Talbot McNaver!" the Duke exclaimed. "It is hard to believe that he would do such a thing, despicable though he is!"

"You know him?" Isa asked.

"Talbot McNaver is not only my cousin," the Duke replied, "but he is also, until I have a son, my Heir Presumptive."

"But of course! I have heard talk of him," Isa said, "but I thought that he lived in England and never came North."

"That is what I thought too," the Duke responded, "but obviously we are both mistaken."

Because she was curious, Isa said in a more pleasant tone of voice than she had used until now,

"Tell me about him."

The Duke, who had been standing, now sat down in a chair.

"Talbot has been a trouble to his parents ever since he was born. He has always hated me because I was more senior in the family than he was."

He gave a little sigh as if he was looking back into the past before he went on,

"He used to torture me when we were children and later did everything to discredit me first with the Clan and then in London when I went there."

"He sounds horrible," Isa murmured.

"Fortunately for me, because he has the reputation of being a rake, only a few people listened to him," the Duke continued. "He hates Scotland and it must be ten years since he left here."

"Then the Englishman somehow found the map that shows the whereabouts of the treasure and brought it to him," Isa suggested.

"That, of course, is the reason for his return," the Duke replied.

"If he is your heir, then that is why he wishes to dispose of you."

"I did not think that he would go to such lengths as to murder me," the Duke remarked.

"But, as he said," Isa pointed out, "it is easy to have an accident on the moors or to fall from one of the towers of The Castle."

"I refuse to be intimidated by Talbot," the Duke stipulated firmly.

"I don't suppose that he would do the deed himself," Isa pointed out. "Do you think he has any followers in the Clan?"

The Duke made an expressive gesture with his hand.

"There are black sheep in every community and, if Talbot is prepared to pay, there are always men like Rory, whoever he may be, ready to accept it."

"Then you must be very careful, Your Grace."

The Duke looked at her with a smile before he said,

"I thought just now that you would be as eager to dispose of me as Talbot McNaver is!"

"Like Your Grace, I do *not* accept insults easily!"

Unexpectedly they both laughed.

"What can I say to you?" the Duke asked. "How is it possible that you can look like you do and apparently, according to Lord Lovat sing like an angel, and yet be prepared to save my life?"

He looked at her for a moment before he added,

"And perhaps find the treasure that has evaded us for so long."

"It would be very disappointing," Isa said in a low voice, "if it did not exist as it is something I have believed in ever since I can remember, "

"And you have searched for it?"

"I told myself stories that I had discovered it in the back of one of the caves or found a trap door under the heather that led me down a long and twisting passage to where it lay at the bottom of it."

The Duke laughed.

"I believe I told myself much the same stories and I remember searching The Castle with my friend Harry just in case there was a secret entrance that had been overlooked."

"The story goes," Isa stated, "that the Chieftain and the Elders were coming back to The Castle when they were shot down by Viking bowmen."

"Which suggests, of course," the Duke said, "that the treasure was hidden on the moors. Well, we have also looked for it there."

He spoke with a note of amusement in his voice, but Isa said seriously,

"On the map which your cousin has given to Rory, it indicated that the treasure was even nearer than where they were looking in the garden."

"If that is where it is, I absolutely refuse to have my flowers and my shrubs, which I have taken a great deal of care over, torn up!"

He sounded so indignant that it made Isa laugh, and once again he was laughing with her

"Are we really sitting here in the middle of the night," he asked, "worrying ourselves over a treasure that has lain hidden for hundreds of years?"

He laughed again and added,

"In fact it may easily have been dissipated by the Chieftain on riotous living and the whole idea of it being hidden from marauding Vikings was just a ploy to exonerate himself from blame."

"Now you are being cynical again," Isa told him without thinking.

"Again?" the Duke questioned.

She looked away from him because she was shy.

"Do I really appear cynical to you?" the Duke asked.

"The word I was using to myself was 'contemptuous'."

"That is not true!"

"I think it is, Your Grace! You were contemptuous of my sneaking into The Castle on a pretence, simply because I wanted to attend your ball."

"And now, of course, I realise that you have attended a number of balls in London," the Duke said.

"A few, but not so magnificent as the one this evening," Isa answered truthfully. "How could they be when they did not dance the reels?"

"I have never seen them danced quite so gracefully as tonight," the Duke said.

She knew that it was a compliment and, because it made her feel a little embarrassed, she rose to her feet.

"I think, Your Grace, I should go to bed," she said. "We will gain nothing by talking any further now over what has happened. All you can do is to be on your guard and perhaps it will be possible to find out if your cousin was in the vicinity tonight."

"I will doubtless be able to tell you that at breakfast," the Duke replied.

He rose as he spoke and almost mischievously Isa looked up at him as he towered over her and asked,

"Are you really expecting me to stay?"

"Not only shall I be angry if you leave, but it might start a whole string of questions that inadvertently might lead someone into being aware that you were in the garden tonight."

Isa's eyes widened and he added,

~90~

"If I have to be careful, so must you. As you are well aware, all through history informers receive short shrift whenever they are discovered."

As he spoke, quietly and gravely, Isa gave a little shiver.

Then she forced herself to smile and say lightly,

"I am not afraid!"

"Of course you are afraid," the Duke contradicted her, "as any reasonable person would be. In their desperate greed for money, men will do anything to gain their objective."

He paused before he continued,

"I feel sure my Cousin Talbot would give his right hand to possess the treasure of the McNavers."

"Is he really as wicked as all that?" Isa asked and her voice was little more than a whisper.

"He is worse!" the Duke replied. "That is why we must both of us be very careful."

Without really thinking and because he was speaking so seriously, Isa put out her hand towards him as if she sought protection.

The Duke took it and then slowly with his eyes on hers raised it to his lips.

"Thank you," he murmured. "I am deeply grateful."

For a moment it was impossible for Isa to move – her eyes were held by the Duke's and neither of them could look away.

Because she felt unexpectedly shy and uncertain of her Feelings, she took her hand from his and walked towards the door.

As she opened it, she looked back and realised that he had not moved from where she had left him, but was standing watching her.

Again their eyes met and she felt that they spoke to each other without words.

Then she was running down the passage towards the staircase that would lead her up to the next floor where her bedroom was situated.

Or was she seeking sanctuary for herself?

*

When Isa awoke the next morning, she could hardly believe that it had happened.

Yet there was her tartan skirt and her velvet jacket lying on the chair where she had left them after she had undressed.

So it was true that she had started to go home and had overheard the three men plotting, as she had heard them before.

'Where could the treasure possibly be?' she wondered.

She was then suddenly afraid that Talbot McNaver would find it, spirit it away and they would never know the end of the story.

Her maid had not yet called her, but she lay thinking and trying to remember everything that she had ever heard about the Duke's cousin.

Then she supposed that if he had been talked about she had not been particularly interested enough to listen.

When she was dressed she went down to breakfast feeling a little embarrassed at seeing the Duke.

It seemed impossible, after she had been so incensed with him and so angry at his insults, that they could have talked together so intimately in the drawing room.

She had known when he kissed her hand that she had experienced a strange little quiver within herself.

It was a sensation that she had never known before.

'I will not be frightened of him, even though he is still overwhelmingly autocratic,' she told herself as she walked towards the breakfast room.

Yet she knew that fear was not exactly what she felt about the Duke at the moment.

There were quite a number of gentlemen seated round the breakfast table, but only two women and they were both elderly.

It was Harry who sprang to his feet to take her to the sideboard.

He found her a plate and lifted the silver tops of the entrée dishes so that she could make a choice of what she wanted to eat.

The Duke was sitting in his familiar place at the top of the table.

He had half-risen as she entered and only when she sat down at the table did he say,

"I hope you slept well."

"I was tired after so much exercise last night," Isa replied lightly, "and I have never, Your Grace, enjoyed the reels more, or heard pipers play better."

"You must tell them so before you leave," the Duke remarked.

Two of the men who were going fishing rose from the table to be off to the river and it was Harry who waited until Isa had finished eating before he said,

"Bruce wants to speak to you. Shall we go into the study?"

The Duke's special room was exactly as Isa would have expected it to be.

There were paintings of stags, grouse and dogs on the walls, several large bookcases and some comfortable leather armchairs, which were very masculine.

Isa walked in followed by Harry.

The room was empty and she guessed that the Duke was saying 'goodbye' to several guests who were leaving early.

"Bruce has already told me what you overheard last night," Harry said, "and I understand that you have identified Talbot McNaver."

"Tell me about him," Isa suggested. "I was thinking this morning that I knew little about him."

"He is utterly despicable," Harry answered, "and has been something of a nuisance as well as an embarrassment to the family ever since I can remember."

He looked at her for a moment before he went on,

"The Dowager Duchess speaks of him with horror, as well she might, and I have often thought that, if Talbot could kill Bruce without being hanged for his crime, he would not hesitate to do so."

"Then what can we do about it?" Isa asked.

"Bruce has sent two of his staff whom he can trust to discover where Talbot is staying. The mere fact that he is in the neighbourhood without anybody in The Castle being aware of it is suspicious in itself."

"Is it certain that it is the Duke's cousin?" Isa asked. "After all, Talbot is a common name in Scotland and there must be quite a number of Talbot McNavers."

"I doubt if any other member of the Clan would be brave enough to speak openly about disposing of their Chieftain," Harry pointed out.

Isa knew that this was the truth and they were both silent until the door opened and the Duke came in.

She thought that, wearing an ordinary tweed jacket over his kilt and a plain sporran made of otter, he still looked magnificent.

When he smiled at her, she had the strange feeling that the sun had come out.

He walked to the fireside.

Then, as if he was making an important announcement, he began,

"You are quite right, Isa. Talbot McNaver is staying somewhere on the Strath and my men are making enquiries as to which of the Clan he has inveigled into his plot. But the whole thing sounds to me like a story for schoolboys!"

The Duke laughed and Harry said,

"For God's sake, Bruce, this is not a joke! You know as well as I do that Talbot hates you, as he always has, and if he is deeply in debt, as I am told he is, then the one thing that would restore his fortune would be to get rid of you."

"Isa has already told me to be careful," the Duke replied, "but short of locking myself away in one of the towers, I cannot think how I can avoid being shot in mistake for a stag or drowned if my boat springs a leak on the loch."

"You could at least swim in the latter circumstances," Harry said, "unless by some mischance you are pulled down by somebody swimming underwater!"

Isa gave a little cry of horror.

"You must not think such things," she asserted. "Perhaps they will be carried on the wind and give Talbot McNaver ideas that he has not had before."

"I am trying to frighten Bruce into being sensible," Harry said. "I know his cousin and if there is one person I know to be a crawling poisonous reptile, it is he!"

"All this is getting us nowhere," the Duke said quietly. "What do you suggest we do?"

"I think," Isa said, as Harry did not speak, "that first we should warn your gardeners and the people in the house to be on the lookout for strangers searching round The Castle, and question them."

She paused for a moment to glance out of the window.

Then she went on,

"Last night was an exception since, because of all your guests, they could move about unnoticed. Today they should be watched and apprehended."

"That is sensible," Harry said approvingly. "Perhaps if we questioned Rory McNaver himself we might learn something."

"We would have to find him in incriminating circumstances," the Duke suggested. "There must be dozens of McNavers in the neighbourhood christened Rory."

"For the first time in my life," Isa said, "I am questioning whether it is a good thing for all Clan members to have the same surname."

"I cannot remember when I have met an 'Isa' before," the Duke remarked, "and 'Isa of the Isles' is a very pretty name for you to use on the stage."

"The Concert platform," Isa corrected him automatically.

Harry's eyes twinkled.

"I apologise," the Duke said. "Please forgive me. Of course I realise the difference and the gulf that exists between them."

"That is something my father would wish you to think."

"Have you told your father what is happening?" the Duke asked.

Isa shook her head.

"It was the first thing I thought of doing, but then I was afraid. My father and mother are both old and very vulnerable, living so far from another house if anyone wished to harm them."

The Duke suddenly gave an exclamation that was like an explosion.

"This is intolerable!" he cried. "How can we sit here being frightened by a creature like Talbot? I think the best thing I can do is to send for him, wherever he may be, and ask him what the devil he is up to!"

"What good would that do?" Harry asked quietly. "He would only defy you, declare, of course, that Miss McNaver is a liar and use the first opportunity he has of finding the treasure of getting rid of you."

"There must be something we can do," the Duke persisted.

"I think Mr. Vernon is right," Isa interposed. "It would be a mistake to take action too soon. Because I realise now that somebody like your cousin would be a disaster as Chieftain of the Clan, you must, for everybody's sake, stay alive."

"You said just what I was thinking," Harry approved. "So, Bruce, there is no question of your going on moors for the next week or so and, if you go fishing, it would be safer to be accompanied by at least two ghillies and a friend like myself."

"The whole thing horrifies me!" the Duke said sharply.

Isa rose to her feet.

"I should go home."

"That is impossible," the Duke said.

"I agree," Harry asserted. "What I suggest you both do this morning is to have a good look round the garden and see if by any chance you can find what that man Rory missed."

He paused to say slowly,

"It will seem quite natural for you, Bruce, to be showing your guest the Water Garden and the cascade and, of course, your flowers. Moreover, because it will be new to her, perhaps Miss McNaver will notice something that has escaped us."

"Very well," the Duke replied. "Durham and my friends from London will be leaving in half an hour and then, Isa, you and I will saunter leisurely in the sunshine."

"I am going down to the river to try to fish," Harry said. "But I will be back for luncheon and after that, if Miss McNaver wishes to return home, I will be on guard. The one thing you must not be, Bruce, is alone."

"Oh, really – !" the Duke started to expostulate, but Harry said firmly,

"That is an order. Neither Miss McNaver nor I will even argue with you about it!"

The Duke laughed a little ruefully.

He then went off to say 'goodbye' to Lord Durham and to his grandmother who was returning to her own house, which was a few miles further North.

Isa went from the room to change the shoes that she had been wearing for breakfast.

There were several other members of the house party who were leaving as well as Lord Durham and they were taking the Duke's private train, which would carry them as far as Inverness.

She thought a little wistfully that one day she would like to travel on the Duke's train herself.

It certainly would be quicker than the uncomfortable old carriage with the slow horses that her father had sent to meet her when she came from the South.

Then she told herself that once he had dispensed with her services for the discovery of the treasure, the Duke would never think of her again.

He would also doubtless forget his promise to invite her father and mother to The Castle.

She waited at the top of the broad staircase until the last guest had gone and, when the Duke had seen them off, he looked up and saw her.

"Come along, Isa," he said, "I can now show you the Rock Garden as I promised to do. I am sure that you will find it very attractive."

He was speaking loudly, she knew, so that the servants who were in the hall could hear him.

She ran down the stairs eagerly to join him.

They walked across the lawns and then down some steps, because The Castle was built on the highest point of the land, which led them towards the burn.

There was quite a lot of water in it, although Isa guessed that when the rains came it would be in a spate rushing into the sea.

The burn would then become a small torrent and perhaps flood over the lower part of the garden.

Everything, however, had been done to direct the source of the water into a series of smaller streams until it reached the cliffs.

What made the Rock Garden so delightful was that it was completely protected by fir trees.

Having inspected the lower part where there were a great number of plants that the Duke had brought from abroad, they climbed slowly up towards the cascade.

As they drew near to it, Isa stopped and said,

"It's so beautiful!"

She was speaking the truth, for emerging from between two high rocks, the cascade, flowing unceasingly, was shimmering in the sunshine.

The water was swirling round a little island of brilliantly coloured plants, dividing and then re-joining the main stream.

As she looked at it, the Duke asked after a moment,

"What are you thinking?"

"I have just remembered a story I once read," Isa replied. "It described how some of the men who fought with Bonnie Prince Charlie hid from the British troops behind a cascade which was rather like this one and were never discovered."

"I think I must have read that story too at some time in my life," the Duke said with a smile.

"Have you ever explored it to see if you can get behind the cascade?" Isa enquired.

"It never struck me it was possible," the Duke replied. "Shall we go and have a look?"

It flashed through Isa's mind that perhaps that was where the treasure had been hidden all those centuries ago.

She thought, however, that the Duke might think it a childish idea.

She therefore kept silent as they climbed up the rough rocks until they were close beside the cascade.

Now it was flowing deafeningly down beside them.

It was then that Isa realised that there was just enough room behind the screen of water for somebody to squeeze past without getting wet.

She pointed it out by sign language to the Duke, for it was quite impossible to speak above the roar of the cascade.

The Duke nodded and smiled.

Holding very carefully onto the rocks she eased her way through a small aperture into what she realised was a cave.

It was larger than she expected. Then as she turned to see the water pouring like a veil between herself and the sunshine, she thought that it not only very beautiful but also very exciting.

She was still staring at it when the Duke, moving as carefully as she had, joined her.

"I cannot think," he said, "why I was not aware of this before. I suppose it is because as a boy I was warned of the danger of going near the cascade in case I was swept away into the sea."

He had to shout for Isa to hear what he was saying.

She laughed and, feeling that she must not miss anything while they were there, she turned round and moved towards the back of the cave.

It was easy to see that the cave was far deeper than she anticipated and because she was curious she walked to the far end of it and the Duke followed her.

It was not high enough for him not to have to bend his head.

But when they had gone for quite some way he said,

"I think in a moment we shall have gone far enough. If we want to explore further, we must come again with a lantern."

Isa stopped when he spoke to her and she realised that they were now the length of a large room from the cascade.

Yet there was still, unless she was mistaken, some way to go.

"It seems a pity to turn back," she said. "I cannot imagine why you have never known of this place before."

"I suppose because, as I have just said, it was thought to be dangerous. At the same time, I would rather we came back again with lanterns than step into the darkness, which might be dangerous."

"How right you are!" a voice said unexpectedly.

Both Isa and the Duke started and would have turned round.

But at that moment Isa felt her arms pulled behind her and her hands tied together.

She screamed and struggled and then realised that the Duke was fighting violently against two men.

Another was enveloping her whole body with a rope.

For a moment she could hardly believe that it was happening.

Then, as she gave another scream of fear, the man behind her tied a handkerchief over her mouth and gagged her.

He dragged her away while the Duke was still fighting.

The man half-carrying her turned the corner of what she thought was the end of the cave and now she realised that they were in another one.

There was a lantern set in the centre of the floor and it revealed how large and high it was.

However, it was difficult for her to see anything except the face of the man who was carrying her.

He was a Scot, unshaven and rather dirty, who was very strong.

He set her down with her back against a rock and chained her ankles together without speaking.

He then hurried back to where she could hear the Duke shouting, although she could not understand what he was saying.

Suddenly there was silence and a few minutes later three men came in carrying the Duke.

He was silent and she thought in terror that they had killed him.

They laid him down not beside her, but on the opposite side of the cave to where they had put her.

She could see from the way his head drooped forward onto his chest that, if they had not killed him, they had rendered him unconscious.

They had tied his hands behind him as hers had been tied, wound a rope around his body and put chains round his ankles.

But he was not gagged as she was.

She wanted to scream, although it was impossible.

At the same time she was rigid with fear and she could see by the light of the lantern that a fourth man, who she knew now was Talbot McNaver, was looking at them both with satisfaction.

There was just a faint family likeness to the Duke which told her that she was not mistaken in thinking that this was his cousin and his Heir Presumptive.

His face was debauched and there was something repulsive about him that made her shrink in fear when he looked at her.

One of the men who had tied him up was like the one who had carried her and the other was the Englishman.

He was the type that anyone would distrust on sight. There was a shifty foxy look about him with his fair hair and small moustache and a chin that receded into a thick neck.

He was, however, she thought, strong and sturdy, as were the other two men who had fought with the Duke.

They were Scots, but only one of them was wearing a tattered and dirty tartan.

She had the idea, although there was nothing to substantiate it, that they were fishermen.

"You hit him too hard," Talbot McNaver said, "and I want him to hear what I have to say. Get a pail of water and throw it over him."

A man picked up a small pail that was standing on the floor beside the lantern.

He went back towards the cascade and there was silence as the three that were left watched the Duke.

No one spoke and, then just as the man's footsteps could be heard returning with the water, the Duke groaned and with what was an obvious effort, he lifted his head and opened his eyes.

"What – has – happened?" he asked and tried to move his arms, which was impossible.

"Can you hear me, Bruce?" Talbot McNaver asked.

With difficulty the Duke focused his eyes on his cousin as he moved forward into the light of the lantern.

"Oh, it – is you – Talbot!" he said. "Up to your – tricks as usual?"

He spoke slowly and with difficulty, but the words were distinct.

"Yes, up to my tricks, as you say, Bruce," Talbot said. "But this is the last time as far as you are concerned."

The Duke glanced at the rough men standing beside him and asked,

"So you intend to —kill me!"

"Not in the way you might anticipate," Talbot McNaver said with a sneer in his voice. "That would be too good for you! Instead, you are going to die slowly here where no one will find you, and with a charming companion to keep you company."

He was jeering at them, Isa knew, and she only wished that she could tell him what she thought of him.

"I have always hated you, Bruce," Talbot was saying. "But now when I take your place as Chieftain of the Clan, I will speak regretfully of your disappearance and tell your friends how much I miss you."

There was no doubt that he was making every word he spoke offensive and the Duke asked,

"Do you – really intend to – leave us here in a place that I – did not until – now even know – existed?"

"What could be more appropriate than that you should die on your own land?" Talbot asked. "While your servants and friends will search for you, they will never be able to find you."

He smiled evilly and went on,

"Of course, I will spread the rumour that perhaps you have run away with this charming young lady, who will also be missing, a very reprehensible act on the part of the Duke!"

"What I am going to suggest," the Duke said quietly, "is that – while your quarrel may be with me, Talbot, it has nothing to do with Isa McNaver. Let her go. I am certain – that you can swear her to secrecy and trust her word."

Talbot McNaver laughed and it was a very unpleasant sound.

"Do you really think that I am so half-witted and foolish as to trust a woman?" he asked. "You trusted one once and look how she treated you! My dear cousin, I would trust no one with my secrets except my English friend and these two stalwart men who are well paid to keep their mouths shut."

He glanced at the two disreputable men who had tied them up and who now grinned at him ingratiatingly.

Then the Englishman intervened.

"Come on, Talbot," he said. "All this talking is getting us nowhere and we have to get out of this place without being seen."

"That is easy enough, as you are well aware," Talbot McNaver snapped. "You go ahead and I shall say a last fond farewell to my inestimable cousin!"

Then to Isa's surprise the three men walked, not as she expected back to the cascade, but beyond the cavern where she and the Duke were lying.

A few seconds later there was visible a shaft of light in the far distance and it was then that Talbot picked up the lantern and said,

"Goodbye, my dear Bruce! When you are dead, I will come back to take away your ropes so that, if you are discovered, no one will know why you are here except perhaps to disport yourself with a pretty young woman!"

He laughed mockingly.

"You know as well as I do that just as these caves have remained undiscovered and unknown for centuries, so if your bones are found in the year 2,000 AD, they will be a museum piece."

His voice rose excitedly.

"No one will know that it was I who was clever enough not only to discover the cave but also to incarcerate you, my dear cousin, in a tomb that there is no escape from."

He laughed again and added,

"Now you will understand that I am the victor and no longer the insignificant undesirable Talbot you all despise. From this moment, I am the sixth Duke of Strathnaver and how I shall enjoy spending the money that you have been so measly with and making the Clan that has bowed down to you do exactly as I tell them."

He walked a few paces and then turned back.

"Goodbye, my dear cousin! Goodbye pretty lady! May you die slowly! May the worms eat your flesh and your bones rot!"

His last three words were almost a shout and he went off in the same direction as the other men.

Isa could see the light of the lantern like a firefly against the darkness.

There was a shaft of light, as there had been before, which she thought must come from the roof above his head.

She reckoned that he scrambled up and out onto the ground above before there was the sound of a cover or a heavy stone being put into place.

For a moment she was too frightened to move.

When her eyes grew accustomed to the darkness, she could just see a very faint light coming from the first cave beyond which was the cascade.

Then she heard the Duke say very quietly,

"Try not to be afraid! We have to think of some way out of this intolerable situation we now find ourselves in."

He spoke without the slightest hint of panic or agitation in his voice.

But Isa knew even as he spoke that there was no chance of their escaping.

They would die slowly of starvation as Talbot McNaver intended that they should.

CHAPTER FIVE

Isa struggled against her gag, but found that, as it had been tied between her teeth, it was impossible for her to move it.

She wanted to talk to the Duke, she wanted him to reassure her and, most of all, she wanted self-control.

She felt the fear of what was happening rising within her and she was terrified that she would try to scream and choke herself.

Worse still, the Duke would be aware that she had broken down, losing her pride and becoming hysterical.

It was dark in the cave, but there was as she had already noticed a faint light coming from the cascade.

As she sat with her back against a rock that was cold and uncomfortable with her legs stuck out in front of her, she was suddenly aware that the Duke was moving.

She could not see what he was doing and she longed to ask him what was happening but could not speak.

Then, as if he knew what she was thinking, he said,

"I am going to try to reach you and see if it is possible for me to remove your gag with my teeth. At least then we shall be able to talk to each other."

He was still speaking in that calm quiet manner that made her feel as if he was laying a cool hand against her forehead.

She was afraid, desperately afraid and terrified, but she tried to think only of the Duke attempting to reach her.

Again she moved her head from side to side hoping that the gag would loosen. It was knotted behind her head and all she succeeded in doing was to make it pull her hair.

She could hear the chains around the Duke's feet rattling and she realised that he was rolling himself over and over on the ground towards her.

She knew because the floor was rough that he would find it painful.

She longed to tell him not to worry, but instead to think of how they could escape, but still she could feel him edging nearer to her until he bumped against her outstretched feet.

Then she saw that he was trying to sit beside her, but it took a very long time.

She was sure that it was about half an hour before finally, although he was unable to use his hands, she felt his shoulder brush against hers.

He had succeeded in doing what he intended.

She could hear him breathing quickly, as if it had been a tremendous effort.

Then, when they were side by side, he gave a deep sigh and said,

"So far, so good! But if we roll ourselves into the cascade, I am afraid we may become unconscious on the rocks and be swept out to sea before we can save ourselves."

Once again he was answering a question that was already in her mind.

Then, because she was still very frightened, it was a comfort to feel that he was so near to her and that somehow the vibrations from him were reassuring, although she knew that there was really no escape for either of them.

After he had rested a little while after the exertion of reaching her, he said,

"Do you think you could bend your head towards me so that I can endeavour to undo the knot of your gag?"

She slipped down a little lower and then managed to bend her head in front of where she thought his lips would be.

"Try to keep still," he murmured.

As she did so, she could feel his mouth feeling for the knot in the gag. It was uncomfortable for Isa because of the rope that encircled her breasts and as she had bent nearer to the Duke it felt as if it was cutting into her.

But she wanted to talk to him and she thought that she could endure anything rather than have to remain silent.

Again it was a long time before, as he worked with his teeth on what must have been a very tight knot, she felt at first a faint loosening.

Then, as she moved her chin and her lips, the Duke gave a final tug and she was free.

"You have – done it! You have – done – it!" she exclaimed, and her voice was very hoarse.

"Thank God for that," the Duke said. "Now at least we can hold a council of war."

She felt that he was being very optimistic, but still it was a joy to be able to talk to him.

She turned her head towards him, saying as she did so,

"Thank you – thank – you! That was – wonderful of – you!"

Then, as she finished speaking, to her astonishment the Duke bent his head forward and his lips were on hers.

She thought that she should be surprised or even angry that he kissed her.

Yet in the excitement of the moment it seemed quite natural.

Without even thinking about it, she moved closer to him and her lips responded to his.

Now his kiss was more possessive and suddenly Isa was aware of a strange sensation within her that she had never known before.

It was not just the elation she felt because her mouth was free, but it was something warm and wonderful like a tide moving up within her body, from her heart to her breasts, up until it reached her lips and the Duke's.

Then she knew that it was what she had always thought a kiss would be like!

What was more, because he was kissing her, nothing mattered, not even the trouble they were in or the desperate fear she felt.

He kissed her until they were flying side by side into the sky.

The stars were twinkling above them as they had last night, and the moonlight was moving through her in an inexpressible manner that made it turn from silver to gold and then to flame.

Only when the Duke raised his head and her lips were free did she feel as if he had brought her back to earth again.

"My darling," he breathed. "Could anyone be more wonderful?"

"What – did you call – me?"

"I called you 'my darling'," the Duke replied, "as you have been ever since the first time I saw you."

"But – you– condemned me as a – liar!"

"I was fighting against what I was feeling, but actually I knew that you were the woman I have been looking for all my life."

"You *did* call me – a liar!"

"What I said and what I thought were not what I felt."

"And – what do you – feel now?"

"I feel, although no one will believe me, as if I have reached Heaven," the Duke said quietly. "That is where you have taken me."

"That is– what I – feel too," Isa whispered.

"You have never been kissed before?"

"No – of course – not."

"That I am prepared to believe," he said and she felt that he was laughing at her.

"Was I – so inexperienced – so ignorant?" she questioned.

She was thinking of the beautiful lady who had been sitting beside him last night.

"You are what I have always wanted to find," the Duke answered. "Someone sweet, innocent and unspoilt. But I did not expect her to look like you!"

"Because – I am a – singer?"

"Because of your red hair."

There was a little silence.

Then he said hoarsely,

"Let me kiss you again, my darling. Then we must decide how we can get out of this hellhole."

She lifted her lips to his and he kissed her passionately and possessively.

She thought that if they died together it would not matter and the ecstasy she felt was from Heaven.

The Duke took his lips from hers and said,

"Let me think! I do *not* intend to die to please my cousin Talbot and we have to contrive how we can save ourselves."

For a moment it was impossible for Isa to think coherently.

All she was aware of was that her whole body was pulsating with the wonder that the Duke had given her.

She wanted him to kiss her and go on kissing her so that everything else could be forgotten.

Then she told herself that she must think of him.

It was ignominious for a man of his strength and his importance to be trussed up like a chicken and left to die in the cave.

No one would know what had happened except for the man who had just left them.

Because she was trying to concentrate on their predicament she said in a low voice,

"What – can I – do? Shall I try to – bite away the – knots of your rope as you have done to– my gag?"

"I think it would be impossible," the Duke replied, "and anyway, I could not allow you to spoil your teeth."

Isa laughed and it was a very pretty sound.

"You are thinking of – my teeth," she asked, "while we lie here in – the dark and will – perhaps never – see the light again?"

"And let Talbot win?" the Duke asked. "*Damn him*! I will have my revenge on him for this if it takes a hundred years!"

That was what it might take, Isa thought miserably.

She was aware now as she tried to move how the men, and she was sure that they were sailors, had tied them very securely.

She thought that it would be impossible to escape without a sharp knife to cut them free.

Then there were the chains around their legs, which Talbot McNaver had fastened with padlocks and taken away the keys.

'He was very – certain we would – die here,' she told herself and shivered.

Her shoulder moved against the Duke's, but he was deep in his thoughts and did not notice.

Then he said,

"I wonder if we rolled ourselves towards the cascade and shouted whether anyone could hear us."

"We might – try," Isa replied.

She feared nevertheless that the roar of the water would prevent their voices from carrying.

Alternatively, as the Duke had already said, if they threw themselves into the cascade, the force of their fall could render then unconscious.

They would be swept over the cliffs and drowned before any one would see them.

'What can – we do? What – can we – *do*?' she asked herself in a sudden panic.

Then in a voice that she strove to keep low and quiet she said gently,

"You know – I will do anything you – suggest."

"What I cannot understand," the Duke replied, "is how Talbot discovered this cave in the first place. I have lived here all my life and had no idea of its existence."

"Rory must have found it when he was searching for the treasure," Isa suggested. "Perhaps in the old days – there was a huge stone sealing the entrance they came through and – perhaps now it is concealed under a number of stones or a cairn."

"I suppose that is the explanation," the Duke said, "but it does not help us at the moment."

"You don't – think," Isa said hesitatingly, "that you could – stand up and – force open the – entrance?"

"With my head?" the Duke asked.

She knew then that she had been thinking that he could push it with his arms, but it was impossible.

Also the weight of what Talbot and his minions might have placed on top of the entrance would preclude his doing anything except hurting himself.

"No, no!" she said quickly. "That would only give you a headache or, worse still, perhaps – injure you – and I should have – no one to talk to."

"As I want to talk to you," the Duke said, "and most of all, to kiss you! But we have to be sensible. We have to find a way of escape."

"I am praying – I am praying with – all my heart that we will find one," Isa cried.

"I am prepared to believe that your prayers will be answered, Isa, and I will certainly add mine to them."

The way he spoke told her that he was quite sincere and she said impulsively,

"I cannot – believe God will let you – die when you are so – essential to the – Clan and to Scotland."

"No man is indispensable," the Duke replied a little cynically.

"You are not an – ordinary man," Isa said. "You are our Chieftain, our guide, our shepherd. Think what would happen if you don't return and – your cousin takes – your place!"

"*Blast him!*" the Duke stormed furiously. "May he rot in Hell for what he has done to us, and most of all, my darling, for what he has done to you."

"I am not – afraid because I am with – you," Isa sighed.

Although it seemed incredible, she knew that it was the truth. She was with the Duke and for the moment nothing else seemed to matter.

Then her common sense told her that soon they would be getting hungry.

When night came, trussed up as they were which prevented the blood from flowing freely, they would be very cold.

'Please – God – *please*!' she prayed in her heart, 'how can You let this – happen to us?'

She could visualise all too clearly how by now the household would be beginning to wonder what had happened to them.

She had an idea that it was long after luncheontime and Harry would have returned from the river.

He would wait, wondering what they were doing and perhaps thinking that they had gone from the garden onto the moors.

Aloud she asked,

"How long do you think it will be before Harry wonders if something has happened to us?"

"Knowing what Harry feels about Talbot," the Duke replied, "I think he will be apprehensive when we are not there for luncheon."

"What will he do?"

"He knows the cascade, which we used to visit together when he first stayed with me during the holidays from Eton. But it never struck either of us that we could go behind it."

The Duke was reminiscing as if he looked back into the past and he continued,

"Otherwise we would certainly have hidden in here from the Tutor who was supposed to look after us in the holidays."

"It is – my fault," Isa said in a low voice. "If I had not gone – behind it into the cave – we should have been – perfectly safe in the garden."

"For how long?" the Duke asked. "I am sure that Talbot had the idea of capturing me sooner or later, bringing me here and leaving me to die. I have to admit that it is more intelligent than most of the things he does."

The Duke spoke contemptuously, but Isa thought what was the use? Talbot had won! He had captured not only the Duke but her as well.

Although the whole Clan might search for them, it would never strike any of them that they were hidden so hear to The Castle.

The hours seemed to drag by, the Duke kissed her again and she knew that every kiss he gave her was more rapturous than the last.

She was aware, although neither of them said so, that already they were both hungry and thirsty.

Eventually kissing would not appease the pangs of hunger, and perhaps in his agony the Duke would hate her.

Her prayers intensified.

'Please – God – please hear us and – let us be found – please God – tell Harry– where we are!'

She felt as if her whole being went up to the sky in waves of prayer and that she must storm the Heavens to save the Duke.

'If I die it is of little or no consequence,' she said in her heart, 'but the Duke is – needed. How can You allow – anyone so utterly– despicable as his cousin to – take his place?'

She felt the Duke's lips on her hair and then he asked,

"Are you praying, my precious?"

"I am praying for you. It is so – important that– you should live."

"If you think I want to live without you, you are very much mistaken. I want you and I am not prepared to die."

He paused for a moment then suggested,

"I think what we should do is to move into the cave beside the cascade. Perhaps someone will come searching the garden for us and if we shout for help our voices might be heard."

"It's an – idea," Isa agreed. "Let's do it!"

She sensed that inaction was unbearable for him.

While in a way she was almost content to be beside him, she knew that they must make every effort to escape.

She had the feeling, however, that like her he could think of no possible way that they could save themselves.

He started to move first and she followed him.

It was agony rolling over the rough stony floor and she thought that after more than an hour they had made very little headway.

Yet they had moved from the cave where they had been left to the back of the cave behind the cascade.

Now the roar of the water was almost deafening.

It told Isa more clearly than words that, however loudly they shouted, it would be a miracle if anybody heard them.

The sun was still shining and as Isa looked at the golden veil ahead she was certain that when darkness came it would be very cold.

However close they might huddle together, she and the Duke would soon be shivering.

It was best not to think about it, but to follow him painfully.

She felt the rocks bruising her knees and her arms even through the thickness of her tartan skirt and her velvet jacket.

Ahead of her the Duke lay still and after a moment she asked anxiously,

"Are you – all right?"

"I am exhausted," he groaned. "I suggest we rest for a while, but not against the sides of the cave which I can see are damp."

He had stopped in the centre where the wall was very rough, but Isa thought comparatively dry.

Only with a great deal of difficulty did the Duke manage to edge himself up until he was in a sitting position.

Then, as she rolled over and over to reach him, there was a tender expression in his eyes that was different from how he had looked before.

She moved up beside him, trying to catch her breath after so much exertion and then he said,

"Now I can see you, and you are even lovelier than I remember!"

"How can you say that?' Isa asked. "I must look – awful."

Her hair had become loose as she had rolled over and was falling over her shoulders.

She managed to shake it away from her cheeks and he said,

"I love you not only because you are beautiful but because you are so brave. Any other woman I know would have been screaming and crying by this time."

"What would be – the point?" Isa asked. "In any case I am with – you!"

"As I am with you," the Duke replied. "If we have to die, I would rather it was this way, because we are together, than any other."

"Do you – really – mean that?"

"I don't think that this is a moment when either of us would lie."

He kissed her gently and then they both stared ahead of them at the falling water.

Neither of them said so, but they were aware that the sun was sinking.

"Save us – oh – God – please – *save us*!" Isa murmured.

She felt her prayer was lost in the roar of the water and the walls of the cave seemed to close in on them.

They were buried.

Buried as completely and absolutely as if they had both been laid in their coffins in the graveyard and the soil shovelled on top of them.

She looked at the Duke and saw the agony on his face and knew that he was thinking as she was.

"The only thing to do," he said suddenly, "is for me to throw myself into the cascade and pray that I shall survive long enough to tell them where you are."

Isa gave a little cry of horror.

"How can you think of – doing anything so cruel – so wicked – as to leave me here all – alone?" she asked. "If you died – trying to save me – do you think I would – want to live?"

"I can think of no other way, my darling."

"Then we will die together. I am not – afraid as long as you are – beside me."

"I think mine is the better way."

"But supposing you are unconscious – as you probably will be – then you will be – swept down the burn into the river and – drowned before you – reach the sea. What good will it have done?"

He did not answer and she added,

~128~

"I shall die – very slowly and agonisingly – and then your cousin will – come to take away – my ropes."

The Duke's lips tightened and she knew that he was biting back the fury he wanted to denounce his cousin with.

"We will be – together," Isa whispered, "and now – because the only thing we can do is to pray that by a miracle of God's mercy – somebody will find us – I am going to – sing to you!"

She did not wait for him to answer, but sang very softly in her unique and beautiful voice *Over the Sea to Skye*.

As she sang, she thought that her voice had never sounded better and that every note was a prayer that would reach Heaven.

Only when she had finished did she turn to look at the Duke.

He had an expression of love in his eyes that made her heart turn over in her breast.

"Could anything be more beautiful?" he asked. "And, my darling, I cannot believe that such beauty can be lost and forgotten."

The way he spoke was so moving that she reached forward to lift her lips to his.

Then, as he kissed her, she was suddenly aware that the light from the cascade was not so bright and there was a dark shadow over it.

As the Duke released her lips, Isa gave a cry of horror because they were no longer alone in the cave.

Coming from the cascade, silhouetted against the falling water, somebody was slowly approaching them.

For a moment, with a contraction of her heart, Isa thought that it was Talbot McNaver.

Then a voice called out,

"Bruce! Are you there?"

The Duke gave a cry that seemed to echo round the whole cave.

"Harry? Thank God – it's Harry!"

He came further towards them.

"You *are* here! I can hardly believe it. I never knew there was a cave behind – !"

He reached them and saw the ropes around their bodies and the chains on their ankles.

"*Devil take it!*" he exclaimed. "What has happened to you?"

"You can see for yourself," the Duke answered.

"You mean – Talbot has done this?"

"Who else?"

"He thought – nobody would ever – find us," Isa told him, and her voice quivered on the words.

Harry crouched down on the floor beside them.

"It's a miracle that I have!" he said in a serious voice. "I have been desperate, absolutely desperate, knowing that some accident must have happened and everyone in The Castle is searching for you."

"But you are here," the Duke said.

"How did you guess – how did you know this was – where we would– be?" Isa asked.

Harry felt in his pocket and said,

"You have to thank something very small and insignificant."

He held something up between his finger and thumb and for a moment the Duke and Isa stared at it, not knowing what it was.

Then the Duke understood and looked down at his sporran.

"Exactly!" Harry smiled. "The eye of an otter. When I saw it glinting at the side of the cascade I thought that it must be a jewel, perhaps something that Miss McNaver had dropped."

"And that saved us!" the Duke exclaimed.

For a moment he closed his eyes and Isa thought that he was saying a prayer, as she was, of utter thankfulness.

"I knew that there must be some reason for it to be there," Harry went on, "and I found the opening behind the cascade."

Then, as if he was aware of how emotional the moment was, he put the little artificial eye from the Duke's sporran back into his pocket and rose to his feet.

"Now stay here while I go and fetch help," he said, "and don't run away!"

"If you are laughing at me," the Duke said, "I will knock you out as soon as I have the use of my arms!"

He was laughing as he spoke.

But Harry was already leaving the entrance to the cave and was squeezing himself carefully through it.

When he had gone, Isa gave a sigh that came from the very depths of her being.

"God has – answered our – prayers and we are – saved!"

"That is just what I was thinking," the Duke agreed. "But I am sure that it was your prayers, my darling, that made Heaven aware of us and brought Harry to our rescue."

"It was the – eye from your – sporran," Isa said beneath her breath. "You must have – scraped it off as you – edged your way – into the cave."

"It is a miracle we shall neither of us forget."

His lips sought hers and he kissed her passionately and now that their crisis was over Isa felt as if she wanted to faint or cry tempestuously.

As if the Duke was aware of what she was feeling, he suggested gently,

"Wait until I can hold you in my arms. You have been brave until now and I would not want any of the Clan to see a McNaver in tears!"

She knew that he was joking to keep her from breaking down.

She gave a shaky little laugh and knew, as he had asked her to do, that she would wait until they were safe inside The Castle.

By the time Harry had summoned two of the servants who could be trusted not to say too much and they had cut the ropes off the Duke and Isa, it was dusk.

There had been a great deal of difficulty in trying to unlock the padlocks to release the chains that encircled their ankles.

As they went back across the garden, Isa was carried by Harry because it was quite impossible for her to walk.

Yet she felt as if there were fireworks flaring in the sky and the whole Castle was emblazoned with light.

But all she could think of was that the Duke was alive and so was she. And for the moment nothing else mattered.

They reached The Castle, and she was carried to her bedroom.

When she had washed, rested and changed from her dusty and stained clothes into a pretty gown, Isa limped to the breakfast room.

There was food for them to eat and champagne to drink.

Both men rose as she entered the room and she thought that the Duke looked even more handsome and attractive than he ever had before.

"I have, with remarkable self-restraint," he said, speaking lightly, "waited for you, but I don't mind saying that I am extremely hungry!"

"You must be starving," Harry said as they sat down at the table.

It flashed through Isa's mind how terrible it would have been to have gone for days without food until finally, thin and emaciated, they would have died in a coma.

As if he knew what she was thinking, the Duke put out his hand and laid it over hers.

"Forget it!" he said. "Just be happy that we are home and I want to tell you that you are the bravest woman I have ever known."

He handed her a glass of champagne as he spoke and Harry said,

"I am going to propose a toast to 'Highland dress'!"

He drank and went on,

"I have often teased you in the past, Bruce, when you were wearing your kilt, your plaid, your jabot, and your skean-dhu. But I will never again laugh at your sporran!"

He finished his champagne as he spoke and Isa said, looking at the Duke,

"I think we must both drink to Harry, who was clever enough to see the otter's eye by the cascade. If the Archangel Michael and all his angels had come to rescue us, I could not have – been more – grateful!"

"I agree with you," the Duke answered. "To Harry! And we are both of us eternally in your debt."

He drank to Harry as he spoke, but his eyes were on Isa and after a moment Harry asked a little hesitantly,

"Am I – imagining things or during those long uncomfortable hours in the cave, has anything – unexpected occurred?"

"What you are asking," the Duke said quietly, "is whether I have yet told Isa that I love her. And I have!"

Harry gave a whoop of joy.

"That is the best news of the day, apart from finding you both," he cried. "I can only wish you every happiness. At the same time, Bruce, *damn you* for having got there first!"

Isa blushed, but the Duke laughed and said,

"If you blush like that, I shall never believe that you are the famous Concert singer that Lovat knew you to be."

They finished their light meal, the Duke saying as they did so,

"I am still quite prepared to eat a large dinner!"

Then they walked out of the breakfast room and, when they reached the hall, he said to Isa,

"I am going to send you to lie down while Harry and I discuss what we should do about Talbot."

She wanted to be with them and to stay with them.

At the same time, she knew that she was tired.

"Do as I tell you," he said quietly. "We will have dinner at nine o'clock, so that there is time for you to sleep."

She went upstairs knowing that he was right and she was really exhausted.

When she climbed into bed, before she fell into a dreamless sleep, she thanked God as intensely as she had prayed for help that they had been saved.

*

Downstairs in the study the Duke said to Harry,

"What do you suggest I do about that swine?"

"I have found out where he is staying," Harry replied, "or at least your Factor has. I intended to tell you at luncheon about it, and was deeply perturbed that you were not here."

The Duke looked at him questioningly as Harry added,

"Your Factor said that Talbot had been seen down at the harbour with two very unpleasant-looking fishermen, who come from the North where they are suspected of being engaged in a number of illegal pursuits, but have not as yet been caught."

"We ought to be able to pin something on them," the Duke said, "although it will be difficult without publicising exactly what has happened, which, to tell the truth, would not show me up in a very good light."

"That is true," Harry admitted. "It would be a great mistake for this to get into the newspapers."

"That is the last thing I want," the Duke replied. "But I was actually thinking of the Clan."

"Who expect you, of course, to be a Knight in shining armour," Harry said mockingly.

"They would certainly not expect me to allow myself to be trussed up and, except for your cleverness, left to die within a few yards of The Castle, while Talbot took my place as Chieftain."

There was a note in his voice that told Harry how much it angered him and he suggested,

"I think the best thing to do would be to say nothing about it at the moment. At the same time Talbot might strike again."

"Not for a week at least," the Duke said.

"Why not?" Harry asked.

"Because he is waiting for me to die of starvation first. Then he will be certain of taking my place as Duke and Chieftain and it will only be a case of my legally being pronounced 'presumed dead' before he becomes the sixth Duke."

"I see your reasoning," Harry responded.

"What we have to do is to make his followers desert him," the Duke went on, "and the best way to do that is to make sure that he has no money to pay them with."

"Now you have given me an idea," Harry said.

They started talking earnestly while Isa, with a smile on her lips, slept peacefully until it was time to dress for dinner.

CHAPTER SIX

Just before Isa left her bedroom to go down to dinner there was a knock on the door and the old maid who was dressing her went to answer it.

There was a conversation in low voices outside which Isa could not hear.

Then the maid came back to her side to say,

"His Grace's compliments, miss, and you'll be dinin' in the small writin' room.

Isa looked surprised, but she thought that it would be a mistake to ask questions and a few minutes later she went down the staircase to the first floor.

The writing room was, she knew, beyond the Duke's study, a room kept for guests staying in the house who wished to write letters.

She entered the room to find that the two men were there, the Duke looking resplendent in his evening clothes with a lace jabot at his neck.

Harry looked less smart but, she thought, more comfortable in a velvet smoking jacket frogged with braid.

She was surprised to see the table laid in the centre of the writing room with silver candlesticks and some of the Duke's exquisite pieces of silver.

The Duke put a glass of champagne into Isa's hand and said,

"It was Harry's idea that we should dine here and he has a very good reason for our doing so."

Isa waited and he went on,

"Harry thinks it essential that Talbot should not know that he has failed in his attempt to kill us."

Isa's eyes widened in surprise, but she did not speak and the Duke continued,

"I have therefore made certain that no one in The Castle will talk about our safe return and we will keep out of sight as much as possible until Harry has put his plan into action."

Isa looked at Harry curiously, but at that moment the servants came in to serve the dinner and the conversation ranged over a great many subjects except anything to do with Talbot.

She noticed after a little while that they were served only by the old retainers who had rescued them from the cave.

She was eager for the dinner to be finished so that she could learn what was to happen.

The table they had dined at was lifted out of the room and she sat down in a comfortable chair by the fire.

She saw that there were several vases of flowers which she was sure was not normal in this little-used room and she thought that the furniture too had been rearranged.

She looked enquiringly at the Duke.

He smiled at her with such an expression of love in his eyes that she forgot everything except that her heart had turned a somersault.

She wanted above everything else that he should kiss her again.

She was thinking how wonderful it would be for him to do so, when he could now hold her in his arms as he had been unable to do in the cave.

Then with what she guessed was an effort he looked away from her and said,

"Now, Harry, you must tell Isa what you are planning."

Harry rose from where he had been sitting to stand with his back to the fire and began,

"You will realise, as I do, that to protect Bruce in the future, we have to catch Talbot red-handed and make certain that he does not continue with his determination to become Chieftain."

Isa gave a little cry of horror.

"Are you saying that we cannot get him convicted of attempted – murder and sent to – prison?"

"Bruce and I have talked it over," Harry replied. "First of all it would entail a great deal of unpleasant publicity. Secondly the only witnesses to his crime are you two, who are most vitally involved, and myself, who did not actually see Talbot truss you up and leave you to die."

This was something that Isa had not thought of before, but now she was intelligent enough to realise that Harry was speaking the truth.

It would be difficult to get Talbot convicted on such slim evidence.

"You will understand," Harry continued, "that if we capture Talbot now and confront him with the crime he intended, his confederates will vanish into thin air and, if we do hold them, they will deny that they were involved."

Isa clasped her hands together.

"Then what – can we – do?" she asked in a frightened voice.

She knew as she spoke that she was desperately afraid for the Duke.

Having heard Talbot McNaver railing against him and the spite and cruelty in his voice when he condemned him to die, she knew that he would not give up.

Of course he would go on fighting both to take the Duke's place and to obtain the money he needed so desperately.

The only thing that mattered, she thought, was for the Duke to stay alive.

She put out her hand to him as if just by touching him she could reassure herself that he was there.

"You are not to upset Isa," the Duke said quietly.

"She has to know the truth," Harry countered, "and perhaps she will make you more careful than you have been up until now."

"I am – afraid for – him," Isa stammered, looking at the Duke and his fingers tightened on hers.

"Harry saved us by a miracle," the Duke said, "and I cannot believe that, now you and I are free, we cannot help him outwit anyone so despicable as my cousin."

"It is not a relationship you can be proud of," Harry said. "Quite frankly, I shall not feel that you are safe until he is dead!"

The Duke did not reply and after a moment Harry said speaking to Isa,

"Now what I have planned is that first thing tomorrow morning, a trusted servant will go to where Talbot is hiding and tell him quietly and seriously that he is wanted at The Castle."

"You will ask him to come here?" Isa questioned in horror.

"I have to assume that, because we have sworn everybody to secrecy, he will not know that you and Bruce have escaped. He will therefore suppose that he has been asked here so that he may be informed that the Chieftain is missing."

Isa drew in her breath, but she did not interrupt and Harry went on,

"I will then confront him with both of you and watch his reaction. Then instead of proclaiming his guilt to all and sundry, Bruce has a proposition to put to him."

"I am going to suggest," the Duke said, "that I pay his debts and give him a generous allowance, if he lives abroad."

"Abroad?" Isa murmured.

"Anywhere except Scotland or England," the Duke replied.

"And what if he – refuses?"

He was silent and she realised that this was a possibility that neither the Duke nor Harry had considered.

"After that, we will have to play it by ear," Harry said. "To begin with I do not trust Talbot further than I can throw him and, if it was possible, I would challenge him to a duel."

"Doubtless he would trick you," the Duke said, "and perhaps kill you."

"We have to do something," Harry pointed out, "and more important than anything else is to make him convict himself out of his own mouth or else make a move that will definitely enable us to bring him to justice."

The eyes of the two men met.

Isa knew without being told that they were both thinking that Talbot would try to shoot the Duke or kill him in some other way.

Then there would be no escape for him.

"It is too – dangerous," she said, as if they had spoken aloud of what was in their minds.

"There is no alternative," Harry replied. "Bruce cannot go for the rest of his life with a bodyguard constantly at his side."

"That is something I utterly and absolutely refuse to do," the Duke emphasised firmly. "As I have already said, the sooner we face up to Talbot and come to some sort of decision with him the better."

"I agree with you," Harry said quietly. "At the moment I would not wager a shilling on your living to be an old man."

Again Isa gave a little cry and then frantically because she was so afraid she turned to the Duke,

"Suppose you went – abroad for a short – while and let everything calm down? And perhaps your cousin will be put in – prison for some – other crime and you will at least be – safe while he is – there."

"That is not practical," Harry claimed.

The Duke lifted Isa's hand to his lips and said softly,

"I am grateful that you should worry over me. At the same time I am convinced that Harry's plan is the only way."

"But – suppose," Isa cried, "when he finds – you are alive – he fires at you – before we can prevent him from – doing so?"

"I shall be ready for any sort of violence that he is foolish enough to attempt," Harry said before the Duke could speak.

He moved from his position in front of the fire to sit down in an armchair beside her and added,

"I am utterly convinced that the only thing we can do is to act quickly and take Talbot by surprise."

"But – suppose – "

"As he took you!" Harry interrupted. "If my plan fails, then we must think again. But for the moment, since we hope and believe that he thinks you are his prisoners, we have the upper hand."

Isa looked indecisive and the Duke said,

"Harry is right, my darling."

There were a number of points she wanted to make, but she was, however, aware that neither man would listen to her and that they had already made up their minds.

With an effort she rose to her feet.

"I think," she said, "I would like to go to bed. I am very tired and will need to be quick-witted in the morning."

She looked at the Duke as she spoke and he knew that she was trying to think of some other way that she could save him if they could not outwit Talbot.

He rose and put his arm around her.

"You must be exhausted," he said gently, "and I have told Harry how brave and wonderful you have been."

Harry walked towards the door.

"I am just going to see that there is no one about who could find out our secret," he said. "Wait here while I make sure that the coast is clear."

He went from the room, but actually Isa felt that his purpose was tactfully to leave them alone.

"Now I can tell you," the Duke said, "a little more eloquently how much I love you!"

He did not wait for her reply, but drew her almost roughly against him and kissed her as if he was afraid that he might have lost her.

For a moment his lips were painful.

Then, as he became more gentle, yet still insistent and possessive, Isa felt as if he was carrying her as he had before up into the sky towards the stars.

The moonlight enveloped them both and the glory of it was like the Divine touch of God.

'I love you! I love you!' she wanted to say, but she knew that there was no need for words.

Her heart was beating against the Duke's heart as she felt an ecstasy seeping through her body and knew that he was feeling the same.

It was all so perfect and so wonderful that she could hardly believe it was real and that she was not dreaming.

Then, when she thought that no one could feel such rapture and still be alive, the Duke raised his head and looked down at her with a tenderness that she had never imagined she would see in his eyes.

"How soon can we be married?" he asked. "I am afraid to let you out of my sight."

She wished that they could be together through the long hours of darkness and did not have to be separated.

"Soon – let it be – very soon," she whispered in reply to his question and sensed that it was what he wanted to hear.

*

When Isa was alone in her bedroom with the old maid who had attended to her before, she learned that she was the wife of one of the men who had released them in the cave.

As the maid undid her gown, she suddenly realised that she was staying in The Castle without a chaperone.

She thought that it would shock her mother and she was glad that neither of her parents would know what a terrifying situation she had been in earlier in the day.

Or that she was facing another one tomorrow morning.

The old maid helped her into her nightgown, then, as Isa climbed into bed, she said,

"I dinna ken whether His Grace has told you, miss, but Donald'll be in the room next to yours keepin' guard on you tonight."

Isa looked at her in surprise and asked quickly,

"I hope someone is guarding the Duke."

"Aye, you mebbe sure of that, miss," the maid replied. "Mr. Vernon is in His Grace's dressing room with Andrew outside his door, both of them armed."

Isa gave a little cry.

Then, as the maid extinguished the lights and went quietly from the room, she could hear her speaking softly to somebody next door and knew that it was Donald.

He was the Duke's personal piper who had played his bagpipes round the dinner table on the night of the ball.

She had thought then how strong and muscular he looked and was sure that if he was on guard it would be impossible for anybody to hurt her.

She stayed awake for a little while saying her prayers.

She thanked God again and again not only that she and the Duke were safe but that they loved each other.

How could she have imagined that love would come to her in such a strange and unexpected place?

Yet she loved the Duke with her whole heart.

She fell asleep with his name on her lips.

*

Isa was awoken very early by the curtains being pulled back.

She saw that the dawn was only just creeping up in the sky and pushing away the sable of the night.

There was a mist over the hills and she could see the cascade pouring down in the garden.

She felt herself shiver as she realised how the sound of the water had nearly been the last thing she had heard on earth.

She was conscious of feeling sleepy and rather woolly headed as she climbed slowly out of bed.

Then she remembered that the Duke would be waiting for her and felt herself come alive with an eagerness to be with him and at the same time with an apprehension of danger.

She thought it would be an agony to be in the same room with Talbot McNaver and, when she looked in the mirror, she realised that she looked pale.

Moreover, because she was frightened, her eyes seemed to fill her whole face.

Then she hurried downstairs to the writing room where they had dined to find both the Duke and Harry eating a large breakfast.

They rose as she entered and the Duke enquired,

"You have slept well, Isa?"

"I slept almost from the moment I was in bed," Isa smiled.

"That is what I wanted you to say."

He helped her to the dishes, which had been arranged on a hastily improvised sideboard that had been a writing table.

As there were no servants in the room, Isa asked, "What are our orders?"

"You both know what you have to do?" Harry answered. "Talbot will be shown first into the drawing room where I will meet him and inform him that I have something of importance to tell him."

"You are certain that he will not be suspicious?" the Duke asked.

"The man I have sent to summon him will tell him as gravely and seriously as possible to come to The Castle and I have told him to look worried."

He gave a little laugh before he added,

"As you are well aware, Bruce, no one can look as dour as a Scot if he is feeling dour!"

The Duke laughed and it seemed to break the tension.

"You two will be waiting for him in the Study," Harry went on, "and when I bring Talbot into the room the light from the window will be full on his face. It will therefore be a second or two before he sees you both standing in front of the fireplace."

"You are quite – certain," Isa asked in a low voice, "that he will– not have a – weapon on– him?"

"Before he can draw one from his pocket or wherever else he might conceal it," Harry asserted, "I will kill him!"

As he spoke, Isa realised that he was wearing the same sort of loose tweed jacket that the Duke was wearing over his kilt.

It would be easy to carry a revolver in the pocket of his jacket without anybody being aware of it.

Then, as if she had thought of it for the first time, she glanced at the Duke's sporran. He was wearing the same one that he had worn yesterday and the otter's head had only one eye.

It somehow seemed to reassure her more than anything else.

If God had sent a miracle to save them in the shape of a small glass eye, why should she doubt that He would not save them again?

Harry looked at the clock.

"If you have both finished your breakfast," he said, "I want you to go into the study. I have sent for Talbot to come here as early as possible just in case by chance he learns something which might alert him to the fact that you are in The Castle and not, as he believes, in the cave."

Obediently the Duke rose from the table and put out his hand to Isa.

As she felt the strength of his fingers and the warmth of his hand, she told herself that she would not be afraid, but would trust both him and Harry who loved him.

Harry went ahead to make certain that the passage was clear and they went into the Duke's study.

It was an attractive room, as she had thought the first time she had seen it.

Its pictures of grouse and dogs, salmon and stags were a fitting background for the man who apart from all his other gifts was an outstanding sportsman.

Then she told herself that everything about him was outstanding.

As the door closed behind him, he held out his arms. She ran towards him and he held her close but did not kiss her.

He merely said,

"Because I cannot live without you, I intend, as soon as this horrible interview with Talbot is over, to send for the Sheriff."

She looked at him in surprise, not understanding, and he went on,

"After that we can be married anywhere you wish, but because after what has happened, I could not bear you to leave me, we will be married by consent."

Isa would not have been a Scot if she had not realised what he meant.

To declare that they were man and wife in front of witnesses would mean by Scottish law that they were married legally.

Just for a second she thought that such speed was unnecessary and would perhaps hurt her father and mother.

As if he understood, the Duke said,

"It is, if you wish, something we can keep secret until we can arrange to be married in the Kirk where my ancestors are buried."

Isa gave a little murmur, but she did not interrupt and he continued,

"I will ask your father and mother to come and stay here and we will explain to them why I cannot bear you to leave me. At the same time I want you as my wife and whatever happens you will bear my name."

It was then that Isa understood the reason for his haste and she felt the tears prick her eyes.

He was thinking, she knew, that if after today Talbot should again try to kill him and succeed, she would be provided for generously for as long as she should live.

She would also be the Duchess of Strathnaver.

She was so touched and so moved by his consideration for her that she could only hold onto him.

Hiding her face against his neck she said,

"Please – take care of yourself –I am so frightened – desperately frightened – that I might lose you."

The Duke held her so tightly that she could hardly breathe as he said,

"Pray God that will never happen! But I want to ensure, my lovely one, that never again will you have to earn your living by appearing in public or that your father and mother are not provided for."

"How can – you be so kind – so understanding?" Isa asked.

He put his fingers under her chin and turned her face up to his.

"I am, of course, praying," he said, "that there will be no need for such precautions or unseemly haste, except that I am impatient to have you as my wife."

Then his lips were on hers and there was no chance of Isa answering him.

He kissed her until the room seemed to swim dizzily around them and they were both breathless before there was a knock on the door.

He took his arms from around Isa and said in the same quiet calm voice that he had used in the cave,

"Talbot is here and we must stand in front of the fireplace as Harry directed us to do and try, my precious, not to be afraid."

There was something in the way he spoke that made Isa feel intensely and overwhelmingly proud of him.

He would be just the same, she thought, if he was facing the guns of an enemy Army or the spears of some savage tribe in the jungle.

She forced herself to smile at him.

Then she held her head high as they moved to the side of the room in front of the fireplace.

Since it was a warm day the fire was not yet lit and there was the fragrance of flowers on the air that came from the blooms brought from the Duke's garden.

Because it seemed as if there was nothing to say, they stood in silence.

Then feeling that she must touch him, Isa slipped her hand into his.

Only by the strength of his response did she realise that the Duke was in fact tense and apprehensive about what would happen in the next few minutes.

Then they heard Harry's voice outside in the corridor and a second later the servant on duty opened the door.

Talbot McNaver walked in with Harry following close behind him.

One glance at Talbot told Isa that he had dressed for the occasion.

His kilt was a newer and smarter one than he had worn yesterday.

Instead of a casual tweed jacket he had on a dress coat with silver buttons and a sporran of white sealskin.

It showed that he expected to take the place of the absent Chieftain.

He walked into the middle of the room and Isa thought that before he saw them there was a gleam of triumph in his eyes that were slightly too close together.

Then, as the door closed and Harry came to his side, Talbot turned his head and had his first sight of the Duke and Isa.

For a moment he seemed to be frozen into immobility.

Then the expression of astonishment on his face was almost ludicrous.

He stared at them as if he was seeing some supernatural beings that did not in fact exist.

"Good-morning, Talbot," the Duke said calmly. "We have asked you here for an explanation of what occurred yesterday."

For a moment Talbot McNaver could not speak and Isa could understand that his voice had died in his throat.

Then he said slowly feeling for words,

"I don't – know what you are – talking about."

"That is a lie and you know it!" the Duke said. "You left us to die, but fortunately it is not yet time for you to take my place, as you planned to do."

The Duke spoke sternly, but Isa knew that he was being deliberately provocative.

Suddenly an expression of rage contorted Talbot McNaver's face.

"How the devil did you get out?" he demanded spitting the words at the Duke. "If it was one of my men who ratted on me, I swear I will kill him!"

"Perhaps you will fail," the Duke parried, "just as you failed to kill me. Now, Talbot, I require an explanation before I hand you over to the Sheriff and charge you with attempted murder."

"You would not dare!" Talbot came back. "I shall deny it!"

"I was afraid that you might try to do that, but I have a number of witnesses who will make quite sure that you do not escape the punishment of your crime."

Talbot looked at him wildly.

Then put his hand into his pocket.

Isa thinking that he intended to shoot the Duke moved swiftly in front of him.

But before Talbot could bring a weapon from his pocket, Harry had the muzzle of his revolver in the centre of his back saying firmly,

"If you threaten the Duke, I will kill you!"

With a swift movement and the desperate strength of a cornered rat Talbot turned round, forced up Harry's right arm, which held the revolver and with his other first struck him violently below the belt.

As Harry's revolver exploded, the bullet hitting the ceiling, he doubled up.

Even as the Duke moved forward to stop him, Talbot had reached the door, opened it and Isa could hear him running down the corridor.

It all happened so quickly and, because the Duke was concerned for Harry, he stopped to see that he was all right before following Talbot.

"Stop him!" Harry murmured painfully.

The Duke obeyed, but by the time he had reached the corridor, Isa with him, they saw only Talbot's head.

He was just disappearing down the broad stairway that led to the front door.

When the Duke and Isa reached the open door, there was only a footman to look at them in bewilderment.

He told them that the gentleman was running towards the harbour.

The Duke hesitated and as he did so Harry came down the stairs behind them.

"You are all right?" the Duke asked him.

"I will survive," Harry replied with a twist of his lips.

"He has gone to the harbour."

"Doubtless to find the men who assisted him yesterday," Harry said grimly.

They were joined at that moment by Donald and Andrew, both carrying rifles.

"Follow Mr. Talbot," Harry said sharply. "Catch up with him and prevent him from getting away."

They nodded as if they understood and set off at a sharp trot through the garden, which was the quickest way of reaching the harbour.

Without even discussing it, the Duke, Isa and Harry followed.

They passed through the formal gardens, which ended in a fence that was nearly at the edge of the cliffs directly below the harbour.

By the time they could stand looking down, Isa could see Talbot.

He was talking to the Englishman and the two men who had tied them up in the cave yesterday.

Directly below them Donald and Andrew slipped and slid down the perilous cliff path to the harbour.

Talbot saw them too.

He stared at them wildly and then a moment later he and the three men had swarmed down an iron ladder below which there was a rowing boat.

The two fishermen grabbed the oars while Talbot and the Englishman sat in the stern.

By the time Donald and Andrew had realised what was happening and were running along the quay, the rowing boat was already heading for the open sea.

The two men were rowing feverishly and with an expertise that carried them quickly away with every stroke of their oars.

Now the boat was going further and further out into the open sea and it seemed to Isa that Talbot had escaped and had won again.

Then she realised that Donald and Andrew had reached the far end of the quay at the entrance to the harbour and were each down on one knee levelling their rifles on the boat.

The Duke realised at the same time as she did what was happening.

"No!" he cried. "No!"

There was no chance of either of them hearing him, but Isa knew that he was incensed at the idea of

Talbot, despicable though he was, being killed by one of his own Clan.

There was a sharp crack from both rifles shooting almost simultaneously, but the men went on rowing.

Talbot and the Englishman in the stern both turned their heads but neither of them collapsed.

'They have missed,' Isa thought.

A second or so later the rifles were re-loaded and the second shots rang out.

By now the boat was well out to sea and being tossed roughly by the waves.

The wind had risen during the night and the North Sea was tempestuous.

For the first time Isa was aware that spray was rising high from the waves breaking violently on the rocks below The Castle.

Then, as she heard a third volley from the two rifles, she thought that Donald and Andrew were just wasting their time.

Talbot had escaped and would live to strike another day.

Because she was afraid for the Duke she moved a little closer to him, holding onto his hand and wishing wildly that she could protect him.

She was surprised when he did not seem to respond.

Then she was aware that both he and Harry were watching the rowing boat with an intense expression on their faces that seemed somehow strange.

Isa followed the direction of their eyes and understood.

The boat had listed over at a strange angle.

The men had ceased to row and were crouching on one side trying to avoid the rifle fire.

Meanwhile Donald and Andrew went on firing at the boat.

Suddenly a wave broke over it and it tipped over, throwing all the occupants into the sea.

The now empty boat was drifting half-full of water and was being tossed relentlessly by the waves.

The oars floated away and the three men and Talbot were all in the sea attempting to cling to what was left of the boat.

The Duke and Harry watched in silence.

Then, as first one man and then another, disappeared beneath the waves, Isa realised that they could not swim.

Vaguely at the back of her mind she remembered hearing that fishermen seldom learned to do so. They said that if their ships were wrecked it was better to have a quick death than a long drawn out one.

Now she could see Talbot facing towards the shore and she knew that he was trying to swim back.

A great wave swept over him and for a few seconds he was submerged.

He then reappeared, but only briefly in the swirl of another swelling wave.

It was impossible not to watch and to hold her breath as she did so.

She knew that even if they had tried to save any of the men drowning, it would have been impossible to get there in time.

There was no sign of Talbot's three accomplices, then just another glimpse of him before he seemed to be sucked under.

Now there was nothing to be seen except for some oars being churned over and over by the waves.

Four men and the boat had vanished.

It was then, because what she had seen was so horrifying, that Isa fainted.

CHAPTER SEVEN

Isa came back to reality and found that she was being carried by strong arms.

She looked up to see the Duke looking down at her and with a murmur of contentment moved her cheek closer to his shoulder.

"It's all right, my darling," he said calmly. "It is all over."

"They are– drowned?"

"All of them," the Duke said firmly, "and it is something I want you to try and forget."

He carried her a little further and then set her down gently on her feet.

"Can you walk?" he asked. "I think it would be a mistake to have anyone in The Castle asking what happened."

"Yes– of– course," Isa replied.

Equally she was glad to hold onto his arm.

She could not remember when she had last fainted, but it had been horrible to see the men fall into the water and struggling panic-stricken before they disappeared.

The Duke walked slowly and, by the time they reached the steps up to the front door, she felt almost normal.

"Go and lie down," the Duke said quietly, "I have a lot of planning to do and later I will come and tell you about it."

He helped her up the stairs until she was in the corridor where her bedroom was situated and then waited until she had entered it.

She was in fact glad to be able to put her head down and try not to think about anything that had happened, hoping that perhaps she would sleep.

At the same time she was overwhelmingly thankful that the Duke was safe and his cousin could no longer threaten him.

She fell asleep while she was still saying her thanks to God.

She awoke a long time later, thinking that the Duke was kissing her.

She opened her eyes to find that it was true.

He was sitting on the side of the bed, the sun streaming in through the windows and his lips were on hers.

Because his kiss was so possessive, he aroused a response within her.

Her eyes were shining when he raised his head and her hands went out to hold him, just to be sure that he was really there.

"I love – you!" she sighed and her voice was a little hazy.

"And I adore you," he replied.

He made as if to kiss her again and then checked himself.

"I have so much to tell you," he said, "and there is very little time to do it in! First your father and mother will be arriving at any moment."

Now Isa was wide awake.

"My father and – mother?" she repeated in surprise.

"I sent a carriage for them and the reason why I want them here to stay the night is that you and I are being married in the Kirk tomorrow morning."

Isa felt she could not have heard aright.

"What are you saying – what has – happened?"

The Duke glanced over his shoulder to make sure that the door was closed before he told her,

"Harry has made certain that Donald and Andrew can be trusted not to talk and nobody else except for us three is aware that Talbot is dead."

Isa listened, her eyes on his face, but she did not quite understand.

"It will take several days, perhaps a week," the Duke went on, "before the bodies of the four men are washed up somewhere along the coast."

Isa gave a little murmur as if she did not want to think about it and the Duke continued,

"Talbot was a McNaver and, however despicable he may have been, he must be buried ceremoniously in the churchyard."

He paused and, as if to make his words more impressive, he said slowly,

"But you and I will not be there, for we shall be abroad on our honeymoon!"

Isa gave a little murmur of surprise and he added,

"If we do not get married immediately, I shall have to be in mourning for several months and that, my precious one, is something I have no intention of being."

Isa understood.

If they were married immediately, then the Duke would not have to pretend to mourn his cousin and Heir Presumptive.

What was more, neither of them wished to wait before they could be man and wife.

"Did you say– we are to be– married– tomorrow?" she stammered.

"Early tomorrow morning and our excuse will be that Her Majesty the Queen has sent for me and I do not wish to travel to London without you."

"It– sounds very– impressive."

"Not half so impressive as being married to you, my lovely one, and for us to go abroad together on our honeymoon."

"Can we– really do– that?"

"We are going to do it, unless you no longer love me."

"You know I love you," she declared. "I love you so much that it is – difficult to think of – anything else. At the same time –."

She hesitated and the Duke waited.

"At the same time –." she went on in a very low voice, "I don't think that you– really ought to– marry me."

"Why not?"

"Because you are so important – and so grand. I thought at the ball you would marry somebody as beautiful as Lady Lavinia Hambleton."

"I am marrying somebody far more beautiful," the Duke replied, "someone who has captivated my heart until no other woman exists in the world except one called 'Isa'!"

"Is that– really true?"

"Do you imagine that I would lie to you about anything so perfect as our love?" the Duke enquired.

They looked at each other and Isa knew that he was right and their love filled the whole world and nothing else was of any consequence.

The Duke drew in his breath as if he forced himself back to normality as he said,

"As I don't want to distress your father and mother with the truth, and I am sure you agree it would be a mistake for anybody except the five people involved to know what happened, they will be told the same story as everybody else."

"I am sure that you are right," Isa said in a low voice. "Both Mama and Papa would be – horrified if they knew what had – happened in the – cave."

"We will just tell them that we have fallen in love," the Duke said, "which is true and that, as I have no idea of how long I shall have to be in London, it is impossible for me to leave you behind."

"Is that– true too?" Isa asked.

"You know that every minute and every second I am away from you," the Duke assured her, "seems like a century!"

He bent forward and his lips held hers.

He kissed her passionately and demandingly until with what seemed a superhuman effort he rose to his feet.

"I must go and meet your mother and father," he said, "and then send out messengers in every direction to inform the Clan that we are to be married."

"Do you expect – them all to be – present?" Isa asked in astonishment.

"As many as possible," the Duke replied. "Those who have sheep or cattle to attend to will undoubtedly arrive at The Castle in time for the festivities which Harry is organising."

Isa knew that this was the roasting of an ox and the consumption of a great deal of whisky and beer.

There would also be the pipers playing non-stop until the early hours of the morning.

She was just a little disappointed that she would not be there, but she knew that nothing could be more wonderful than to be alone with the Duke on their honeymoon.

She put out her hand towards him and he said,

"You are not to tempt me, Isa, otherwise I shall stay here kissing you and your mother will undoubtedly be shocked that I am in your bedroom!"

Isa laughed.

It seemed so funny that such a little thing could matter after all they had been through together.

When the Duke had gone, she jumped off the bed to tidy herself in the mirror.

She thought, as she gazed at her reflection, that she looked starry-eyed and, without being conceited, prettier than she had ever looked before.

It was because she was in love and she thought, if it was possible, the Duke was even more handsome than when she had first arrived at The Castle.

She told herself that she would make him happy and never again would he look contemptuous or cynical.

Then, because all she wanted was to be with him, she hurried to the drawing room and she found that her father and mother had already arrived and were staring at the Duke in astonishment as they listened to what he had to tell them.

*

After dinner that evening when Isa's father and mother had gone to bed and only the Duke and Harry were left with her in the drawing room, Isa asked,

"Are you quite certain that– no one has any – idea what– happened today?"

"Talbot was very secretive because he did not wish us to know that he was in the vicinity," Harry answered, "and the only person who might miss him will be Rory, whoever he may be."

"I have made some discreet enquiries," the Duke said, "and I gather he is a disreputable old character who is always begging from somebody. For the last twenty-four hours, having obtained money from some unknown source, he has been too drunk to be coherent."

It was impossible not to laugh.

Then Isa said,

"Do you think it was– Rory who found – the way into the– cave?"

"I imagine so," the Duke replied, "and I am quite sure that Talbot expected to find the treasure there. That is what they were looking for when we surprised them by walking in through the 'front door' so to speak."

"Of course!" Isa exclaimed. "What a surprise it must have been for them."

She gave a little shudder as she thought of the terror she had felt when she had been seized from behind and her wrists tied together.

Then she gave a sudden cry.

"What is it?" the Duke asked.

"I have just thought of something," she answered, "and I cannot imagine why we did not think of it before."

Both the Duke and Harry were listening and she went on,

"I think I know where the treasure is!"

"What do you mean?" the Duke asked. "It cannot be in the cave or Talbot would have found it."

"Not *in* the cave, but *under* it!"

The two men stared at her and she explained,

"I have often wondered if the Chieftain of those days would have hidden the treasure in the loch, but it is too far from The Castle. The map which the Englishman showed to Rory marked the treasure as being somewhere in the garden."

"Go on," the Duke said as Isa paused for breath.

"If there was a hidden cave behind the cascade, as we discovered, why should there not be one, perhaps a very small one, lower down where the water actually falls and strikes the rocks?"

"It's a possibility," Harry agreed.

"Do you not see that even if the Chieftain did not know of the cave," Isa said, "the treasure, most of which must have been unbreakable, would doubtless have been in an iron box?"

"That is true," the Duke murmured.

"It would be too heavy," Isa explained, "for the cascade to wash it away, but strong enough, we hope, to defy the time it has existed either with the water beating directly onto it or, what I think is more likely, to be tucked away behind it at the very bottom of the rocks it falls over."

The Duke looked at Harry and for a moment neither of the men spoke.

Then Harry exclaimed,

"My God, I do believe she is right!"

"I would not be in the least surprised," the Duke agreed. "I am so lucky, so unbelievably lucky to have found Isa, it is as if both the moon and the stars have fallen into my hands at the same time, therefore I accept this as another gift from the Gods!"

He smiled at Isa as he spoke and she knew that, if he was lucky, then she was lucky too.

"The moment you return from your honeymoon," Harry said, "we will investigate. Until then, the treasure can remain quite safely where it has been for all these years."

"If you dare to go exploring without us," the Duke exclaimed, "I shall exile you from my land!"

Harry laughed.

"You need not worry. I intend to be here as soon as you return, catching your salmon and shooting your grouse in the autumn. What is more, being Godfather to your sons!"

Isa blushed and looked shy as the Duke said,

"As my Best Man how could you be anything else?"

*

To Isa it was like a dream when the next morning her mother came early into her bedroom to help her into the beautiful white gown that she had worn at the ball.

She thought that perhaps the décolletage was too low for a bride.

As her mother thought the same, they had lifted the chiffon higher, so that it now looked exactly as a Wedding gown should.

To wear over it was a lace veil that the housekeeper said had been used by every Duchess of Strathnaver for three centuries.

There was also a magnificent diamond tiara that had belonged to the Duke's mother.

"You look lovely, my dearest," Mrs. McNaver said as she kissed her daughter.

"I am so happy, Mama."

"I am happy too," her mother replied, "I could not imagine anyone more charming or more handsome than your future husband. I am sure you will find the happiness that your father and I have always known together."

Her father was a little more reticent in what he had to say.

But Isa knew how proud and happy he was as he took her up the aisle of the small Kirk to where the Duke was waiting.

Isa knew that no man, resplendent as he was in full dress, could look more magnificent and at the same time more romantic.

Despite the short notice, the word of their marriage had obviously been carried on the wind, for the Kirk was packed with Members of the Clan.

Outside there was a crowd who must, Isa thought, have been hurrying to The Castle since the first moment that they heard the news.

The fishing village was actually only a mile away to the North and she was sure that every inhabitant from the oldest to the youngest had come to see them and to wish them good luck.

There was not only the Duke's pipers to play for them as they came from the Kirk, but every McNaver who had pipes of his own was there to make himself heard.

They marched ahead of the carriage as they drove back to The Castle, while the Members of the Clan followed behind.

On The Castle steps the Duke made a short speech thanking them for their good wishes and asking them to drink his bride's health.

Isa saw with amusement that already an ox was being roasted as well as a stag and Harry had arranged for there to be a great number of barrels of beer besides the traditional whisky.

She changed from her Wedding gown into a pretty outfit that she had worn in London.

To travel on his private train to Edinburgh the Duke gave her a velvet cape edged with sable.

"It belonged to my mother," he said, "and you will find it useful when we board my yacht to take us to London."

"We are going by sea?" Isa asked in surprise. "I thought that it would be by train."

"It is easier to be alone with you and certainly more comfortable in my yacht," the Duke said. "If it is rough we can stay in harbour. If not, I think that you will enjoy the voyage as much as I shall."

She knew that she did not mind about anything so long as she was alone with him.

Actually she was a good sailor, having been sea-fishing many times with her father in quite rough weather.

A number of the Clan came to see them off in the train, which was always a source of interest and amusement to them.

As they steamed out of the small private Station, Isa and the Duke stood at the window of the drawing room compartment waving until everybody was out of sight.

She had a last glimpse of The Castle silhouetted against the sky.

It was a symbol to the McNavers that they belonged and their Chieftain would rule them, protect them and fight for them.

It flashed through her mind how terrifying it would have been if Talbot had won his campaign and been installed there in his cousin's place.

Then the Duke's arms were around her and he was guiding her to a comfortable sofa.

"Is it – really true that we are – married and I am your – wife? And we need no – longer be – afraid?" Isa asked.

"I hope I shall never again see fear in your eyes," the Duke said, "or be terrified that we must both die."

As if the agony of what he had felt was still in his mind, he drew her closer to him.

*

There was a great deal of Scotland Isa wanted to see from the train as they travelled South.

One of the Duke's servants served them with a delicious luncheon and there was champagne to drink with it.

There was so much to talk about and so much to tell each other that the journey passed quickly.

They arrived at Edinburgh while it was still daylight and could see Edinburgh Castle, which had always seemed to Isa to be enchanted, high above the town.

From the Station they drove to where the Duke's yacht, *The Thistle,* lay at anchor.

After they had been piped aboard, the yacht began to move slowly down river towards the sea.

The Thistle was a new acquisition and the Duke was very proud to show Isa the lighting that he had installed and the way that he had decorated the cabins.

There were many other unusual features and gadgets which he claimed proudly that no other yachtsman in the North possessed.

They dined in the Saloon, which was decorated in green and had a painting of The Castle on one wall.

It reminded her of the last and impressive glimpse she had had of it from the train that morning.

As she looked at it, she said quietly to the Duke,

"I will try to make it such a happy home that you will never want to leave it."

"Now that I have you, I should not want to anyway," the Duke answered, "and I think, darling, it will be the right place to teach our children all the things that we both believe in."

She gave a little sigh as she said,

"I am sure it was our prayers that brought Harry to us, and if you had not prayed as I was doing, we might – never have been – saved."

"I do not want to think of that time again," the Duke said. "All the same, my darling, I shall never forget that when Talbot threatened to shoot me, you stood in front of me so that you could save my life."

"I-I did not think you – realised that was what I was – doing."

"Because I have not spoken of it?" the Duke asked. "It was so wonderful of you, so unbelievably brave, that I was waiting for the right moment in which I could thank you."

"Is that now?" Isa asked.

"Now, and a little later," he answered.

Because she knew what he meant she blushed.

*

The Master cabin, which the Duke had given over to Isa, was very impressive.

The big bed, with a crimson velvet headboard on which was embroidered the Strathnaver Coat-of-Arms, was in its way very masculine.

The Duke had, however, ordered two huge vases of Madonna lilies, which stood on each side of the bed and their fragrance scented the air.

The Thistle was anchored for the night at the very mouth of the estuary and they would not begin their voyage to England until first thing in the morning.

The Captain had predicted that the sea would be calm and now there was just the gentle lap of the waves against the side of the yacht.

When Isa opened the porthole, there was a taste of salt on the breeze.

The Duke went to the cabin next door and she undressed quickly putting on a pretty and diaphanous nightgown that she had made herself, but had thought it rather revealing.

At the time she had supposed that nobody would see it.

Now because it made her feel shy she slipped quickly into the big bed.

She could feel her heart beating as she heard the door open and the Duke came in to stand for a moment just gazing at her from across the cabin.

She was sitting up against the white linen pillows, which bore his insignia embroidered in the corner.

Her red hair fell over her shoulders.

The Duke knew that he had never seen anything so beautiful as it glinted in the light and seemed almost to have a life of its own.

Her eyes were very wide in her heart-shaped face and he thought that no woman could be so lovely.

At the same time there was something spiritual about Isa that he had never known in another woman.

He moved slowly towards her thinking that now at last there was no need for hurry.

They had their whole lives in front of them and he could savour this moment so that it would always remain in his memory.

He sat down on the side of the bed facing her.

"Have you any idea how beautiful you are?" he asked in a low voice.

"I-I want you to – think so," Isa replied.

"How can I think anything else?" he replied. "The only thing that is hard to believe is that you are mine."

"You are quite – sure I am – what you want?" she teased.

"I want you in a way that there are no words for," he answered. "Perhaps it can only be expressed in music."

She gave him a little smile.

"I will sing to you tomorrow."

"I shall never forget the beauty of your voice as you sang to me in the cave," the Duke answered, "and I shall always want you to sing to me when I am not kissing you."

"My song was – a prayer," Isa said softly.

"I know that," the Duke answered, "and if I never believed in prayer before, I am now utterly convinced that our prayers were heard in Heaven and that made Harry find the small glass eye that saved our lives."

Isa gave a deep sigh.

"Supposing he had not – seen it? Supposing the – sun had not been – shining?"

"These things are pre-ordained," the Duke said, "and because we have been through so much together, it must in some strange way enrich our lives."

Isa gave a little cry.

"That is just what I want you to think and feel. Because we have suffered agonies, we shall understand other people's troubles and be more qualified to help them."

The Duke bent forward to push her back against the pillows.

She thought that he was about to kiss her lips and they were ready for his.

But he looked at her and asked,

"How is it possible that I could find anyone so perfect and so exactly what I wanted in my wife?"

"You have never – told me why you have not married before."

For a moment the Duke did not move and she wished that she had not asked the question.

Then he said,

"It is something that I would have told you before we married, if everything had not been in such a rush."

"I don't want you to tell me, if you would rather – keep it a secret."

"There are no secrets between us," the Duke said firmly, "and what I will tell you will explain why you thought I looked contemptuous, although actually I was thinking how beautiful you were!"

"Then – tell me."

To her surprise the Duke did not answer at once.

He took off the long robe he was wearing and climbed into bed beside her.

She felt her heart throbbing and a little wave of excitement seemed to rise up into her throat so that it was difficult to speak.

The Duke did not touch her, but merely lay beside her and began,

"Soon after I was twenty-one, the family began to plead with me to find a wife. Although I had no idea of it, they were already aware of how unprincipled Talbot was! They therefore wished me to start a family as soon as possible as a precaution against him inheriting."

Isa thought that since he was now thirty-three there had been many years for the family to be perturbed at the idea of Talbot succeeding him.

She did not speak, however, and the Duke went on,

"My mother continually invited marriageable young women to The Castle, but I found none of them matched up in any way to the ideal woman I had in a secret shrine in my heart. I therefore refused even to consider becoming engaged to any of them."

He hesitated as if he was feeling for words.

"When I was in London aged twenty-three, I was introduced to Mavis, who was the daughter of Lord Templeford, and from the point of view of the family was a very suitable wife."

"Was she – very beautiful?" Isa asked.

She could not help a feeling of jealousy sweep over her, knowing that somebody else had captured the Duke's heart.

"I thought at the time that she was the loveliest girl I had ever seen," the Duke said.

Isa wanted to beg him not to tell her anymore because she felt that she could not bear it, but he was already saying,

"There was no need for her beauty and her desirability to be impressed on me by my relations, I was aware of it for myself."

Isa wanted to put her hands over her ears.

Yet she knew that she had to go on listening, even though she felt every word was like a dagger being plunged into her breast.

"I thought that Mavis found me as desirable as I found her," the Duke continued. "She certainly accepted eagerly every invitation my relatives gave her and my mother and father came down from Scotland to open our house in London so that they could entertain her."

Isa clenched her fingers together and the Duke carried on,

"Naturally, you will understand, she was strictly chaperoned, so that I was hardly ever alone with her. We danced together, sat next to each other at dinner and it would have been impossible for any man not to be fascinated by her beauty."

Unexpectedly there was silence.

Then Isa asked in a voice that trembled,

"W-what – happened?"

She had a sudden fear that Mavis might have died, in which case she would be enshrined in the Duke's heart forever.

"Lord and Lady Templeford," the Duke went on at last, "gave a huge house party at their ancestral home in the country. It was quite obvious to me and to everybody else that this was the moment when I must propose to Mavis."

His voice changed as he added,

"Then our engagement would be announced at the dinner that was to take place before the ball. After that it was only a question of setting the date for the Wedding."

"What – happened?"

Isa asked the question because she felt that she could not bear the story to go on any longer.

She was aware that the Duke's voice had altered and there was now a note of hardness in it.

Although she did not look at him, she suspected that the expression on his face was as contemptuous as it had been when she first met him.

"The day before the ball I arrived with my parents to stay with the Templefords," the Duke said, "and Mavis greeted me with a smile and whispered so that only I could hear her, 'I am so excited that you have come'."

He paused for a moment to clear his throat before continuing,

"I was excited to be there and, as we sat together at dinner, I managed to whisper some intimate things under my breath, which she reciprocated in a way that made me believe that she was as much in love with me as I was with her."

Isa closed her eyes.

She was asking herself if she really wished to hear all this on her Wedding night.

She felt now that Mavis would always hold some special place in the Duke's affections that she could never reach.

"After dinner we young people," the Duke was saying, "played some childish games and there was no chance of my talking to Mavis alone. Only when we said 'goodnight' did her fingers tighten on mine as she said in a whisper, 'let's ride alone before breakfast tomorrow morning'."

He paused again before he said,

"I knew then that she had chosen the place and the time. I went to bed with my head in the clouds and found it impossible to sleep. All I could think of was Mavis, her eyes looking into mine, and tell myself how lucky I was that she would be my wife."

Isa wanted to cry out that she would hear no more, but the Duke's voice went on relentlessly,

"Finally, because I was so restless I got up, dressed and slipped out of the house by a side door so that the night-footman did not see me. I thought that I would saddle one of my horses and go riding. So I went to the stables wishing that Mavis could be with me."

There was a long drawn out pause before the Duke said slowly,

"The stables were in darkness, but it was not dark in front of the house because there was a moon. As I walked across the garden towards the stables, I thought that everything seemed enchanted."

He stopped as if he was reliving what he felt.

"Then, just before I reached the entrance to the stable yard, I saw two people standing under the trees. They were out of sight of the house and if I had not taken a detour to avoid being seen in the moonlight, I would have gone directly to the stables and missed them."

Unexpectedly he added,

"I can only thank God, who has always protected me, that I went the way I did!"

"But – why?" Isa asked.

"Under the trees just outside the stable yard I saw Mavis being passionately kissed by a man! "

Isa opened her eyes wide in surprise.

"My first impulse was to rush and protect her," the Duke said. "Then, as he raised his head, I recognised him."

"He was – one of your – friends?"

"No," the Duke said harshly, "it was the Templefords' Head Groom who I had discussed the stabling of my horses with when I arrived."

Isa gave a gasp.

"For one moment," the Duke continued, "I still thought that Mavis needed my protection and that he was assaulting her, but, as I watched them, she put her arms around his neck and drew his head down to hers. He kissed her again and then, as if they had agreed on something, he drew her into the stables."

His voice sharpened as he finished contemptuously,

"Without following them I knew why they had gone there, doubtless into an empty stall where they would not be disturbed!"

Now the Duke's voice was as raw as if the memory of what he had seen still angered him.

"I-I cannot believe – it!" Isa whispered beneath her breath.

"Now you understand why if I thought that anyone was lying to me or if I suspected I was being deceived, I looked what you called 'contemptuous'. "

"You must – have been – deeply hurt," Isa said softly.

"It not only hurt me, it also humiliated me so much that I swore that no other woman would ever humiliate me again, for I would never again trust one."

"I don't – want to think – about you being – unhappy."

The Duke turned round so that he could look at her.

"You understand?"

"Of course I understand – and, my darling husband – I will try and – make it up to you."

"You have done that already," the Duke replied, "and now instead of feeling bitter I can only thank God that I found out about Mavis in time."

He drew nearer to Isa and put his arms around her.

"Suppose I had married her," he said, "and then, which I think was inevitable and pre-ordained, met you?"

Isa smiled.

"You are – always saved at the – last moment."

"I knew you would say that," the Duke said. "Oh, my precious, how can we ever doubt that we were meant for each other since the beginning of time and now nothing and nobody shall ever separate us."

Isa put her arms around his neck.

"I love you," she sighed, "and all I want is that my love shall be enough for you to forget – everything that has – happened in the past."

"Everything!" the Duke asserted firmly.

She knew as he spoke he included his cousin Talbot in that word.

"You are mine," he said. "Now all the ghosts are swept away, all the horrors are forgotten and the only thing we have to think about, my precious, is the future."

"I-I will – try to make – you happy," Isa said. "Please love me – I know if you should ever – desire anybody – else I would want to die!"

"Do you think that is possible?" the Duke asked. "I told you that I thought myself in love with Mavis, but it was only a boy's infatuation for a pretty face. What I feel for you is quite different."

He drew his lingers down her cheek.

"You are beautiful, my darling, more beautiful than any woman I have ever seen, but there is so much more."

He kissed her forehead before he said,

"I adore your courage, your intelligence and there is so much I want to talk to you about and find out if we think the same."

He kissed her eyes and said,

"When I look into your eyes, they tell me that your heart is mine and that it is kind, compassionate and understanding. What man could ask for more?"

Isa laid her cheek against his as he went on,

"You are so soft, feminine and sweet, which is everything I have ever wanted in the mother of my children."

Isa gave a little murmur and he said gently,

"Does that make you shy, my precious? But what could be more wonderful than for me to see you holding my son in your arms?"

She knew that the idea excited him and he went on,

"There is something else that I love about you and that makes you different from any other woman I have ever known."

"What – is – that?"

"It is what you call your soul. You believe in God, you pray, and I know you are intrinsically pure and good. That is what I have always wanted in my wife and thought that I would never find."

"How can you say such – wonderful things – to me?" Isa asked. "Suppose I – fail you?"

"You will never," the Duke answered. "We are both Scots and are therefore 'fey'. So we both know that we are one person and have been since the beginning of time."

He gave a deep sigh.

"You are what I have always been looking for and now I have found you, You are mine. Mine, my precious one, and I could no more lose you than lose my life."

His lips were very near to hers as he said,

"I have told you what you mean to me, but there is one more thing. It is not yet mine and I want you to give it to me."

"What – is that?"

"Your beautiful adorable body! I worship you my perfect little wife. At the same time I want you."

"Oh, darling I am — yours." Isa answered. "And thank you for all the wonderful things you have said to me, which I will — never forget."

"I have a great many more to say," the Duke answered, "but most important of all is that I love you! Tell me you love me too,"

"I love you— *I adore — you*!"

The words came from the very depths of her soul.

The Duke kissed the softness of her neck, giving her strange sensations that she had never known before.

His lips went lower and kissed the hollow between her breasts and she felt herself thrill.

Shafts of fire were running through her body and flicking in her throat and it was so rapturous that it was almost a pain.

"I love you, my darling, my adorable, perfect little wife and you are mine,"

The Duke's voice vibrated with passion.

Then his lips were on hers and he knew as he kissed her and went on kissing her that he was carrying her up into the sky as he had done before.

The Gates of Heaven were open and a Divine Light enveloped them with an ecstasy and wonder that came from God.

It was part of the glory of Scotland, its history, its courage and its hope for the future.

Like the magic of the moors, the beauty of the sea and the music of the birds, it was all theirs.

As the Duke made Isa his, she knew that they had found the priceless treasure of real love, which was both spiritual and human and was theirs for all Eternity.

OTHER BOOKS IN THIS SERIES

The Barbara Cartland Eternal Collection is the unique opportunity to collect all five hundred of the timeless beautiful romantic novels written by the world's most celebrated and enduring romantic author.

Named the Eternal Collection because Barbara's inspiring stories of pure love, just the same as love itself, the books will be published on the internet at the rate of four titles per month until all five hundred are available.

The Eternal Collection, classic pure romance available worldwide for all time.

Made in United States
North Haven, CT
30 September 2023

42186608R00124